THE ADVENTURES OF GABBY

Life, Love, Care, and Sacrifice

J VIGH HERMAN . PHD,

DEDICATION / AUTHOR'S NOTE

Roy T. Bennett once said

"Don't let the expectations and opinions of other people affect your decisions. It's your life, not theirs. Do what matters most to you; do what makes you feel alive and happy. Don't let the expectations and ideas of others limit who you are. If you let others tell you who you are, you are living their reality — not yours. There is more to life than pleasing people. There is much more to life than following others' prescribed path. There is so much more to life than what you experience right now. You need to decide who you are for yourself. Become a whole being. Adventure."

PREFACE

Ever met a cancer patient? Or have you seen or known any one in particular that has suffered from cancer. If you have, then you certainly have an idea of how hard it is for anyone to go through this. The pain these patients experience is not one as relatable as that you get when you have a headache, because not everyone has experienced cancer. Even some that have experienced it in its milder forms have probably experienced the condition in a different part of their body. The point is, many of us have absolutely no idea what it feels like to have cancer. We don't "know how they feel", so how can we even comfort them? How can we be of help when we may still think they are exaggerating their pain?

It is now obvious that more than ever, especially with the increasing tendencies for people to develop cancers, we need an enlightenment on the kind of support a cancer patient needs in every area; while it is financial for some, what others need is simply all the emotional support they can get. As cancers differ, the need of each patient is also different. This book highlights the needs of cancer patients and the kind of attention we can give to really help them in a world where they probably feel alone because no one can exactly relate to their peculiar experience. Here is an insight to the condition of various patients using story-telling to narrate their experiences. They are people like you and me, from all walks of life. They are mothers, fathers, aunties, uncles, sisters, brothers, and friends. They are humans just like you and me. They truly need all the support they can get.

Happy reading!!!

CONTENTS

CHAPTER ONE

I hate hospitals. I hate seeing people sick. I hate seeing them in distress. Oh! The smell of drugs each time you walk through the corridors of a hospital; I hate that too. However, the sight of the doctors, nurses, physiotherapists and every other health professional in white or in scrubs gives me undiluted joy. The sight is one that sticks every single time. More than their outfits, for me, it is the nobleness that the outfit connotes. It is the dedication of every health professional to giving the "hopeless" hope once again. It's in the fact that they are a set of people that devote their lives to making others live better; waking up every morning and knowing that they work they do for money is one that saves lives and brings smiles back to numerous faces.

However, this does not take away my dislike for hospitals. Yet, I for one can say it is not an absolute feeling; it is more like a love-hate relationship; hating a place but loving those who work there. Strange, right? Yeah, quite strange. Since I love health professionals that much, as a kid, I remember going the hospital and hating the smell of the place, then, wondering why these people who I admired so much would enjoy working in such a place. Yes, I have always admired them since I was a kid. They would have smiles on their faces as they walked down halls and a few would be walking down with a sense of urgency—the little me guessed that the sense of urgency was borne out of the need to save a life. Anyway, my little mind quickly figured that they would not be healthcare professionals if they did not work in a hospital. I do not know why it took me a while to figure that out though. Well, kids would always be kids I guess.

This whole situation in my head probably paints the picture of if I would ever like to work in the hospital. Or maybe it doesn't. Well, I never thought of if I would love to or I wouldn't until my cousin, Diane, asked me to cover up for her as a volunteer in the oncology unit of St. Greg's hospital. Now, let me say a bit about Diane. This 18-year-old cousin of mine is purely Caucasian, unlike the Black-American that I am. She is beautiful with light brown eyes, and she is about 5 feet and 8 inches tall. She has a lovely and large mass of black hair too. She has lived with us since she lost her parents many years ago, as her mom and my mom were sisters. So, you can probably figure that I am a black girl because of my dad.

Growing up, Diane had always been the sweet girl, always wanting to do nice things for people, and I am not talking about helping people just in the way any of us do—like helping someone who runs into you pack their books. For Diane, it is usually premeditated. She keeps thinking of new and innovative way to help people in need.

Here's a short story: When we were little, we went to the ice cream shop with mom and on our way there, we noticed some homeless kids looking for the remnants in water bottles from a garbage can. Little did I know that my cousin had felt the whole situation on a different level. All I knew was that she was really sad for the rest of the day. On our next trip to the ice cream shop, she asked permission from mom to take several bottles of water along with her. She said there were some kids who needed it. So, she asked mom to stop by the time we got to their small shelter and gave them the bottles, about five bottles of unopened water. The faces of those kids lit up and although I am not exactly an empath, up until now, I can still remember the sincere smile on their faces. In life, it's really the little things, right? Diane looked fulfilled after giving them water. Her worried look which had lasted for days was now gone. My little mind just formed an image of my cousin in my head; an image that somewhat looked like that of Mother Theresa. Well, thanks to the stories I've heard about her. Mind you, she is only a few months older than me, but I guess we were maturing differently. As for me, at that time when we were about seven years old, I was more interested in knowing about fashion brands and makeup from TV shows. My mom really had to do a lot with calming me down on that level.

There are many other *Diane the empath* stories that I would love to tell, but let's focus on the present day Diane and the offer she has made me.

Well, let's take things back a little bit, so you can understand why working in St. Greg's hospital is being discussed by two teenagers who finished high school a few months back. With the little I have said about her, you should be able to figure that I was not surprised the moment she told me that she had volunteered to be part of a support group for cancer patients. Well, what they essentially do is provide a safe space where cancer patients as well as their caregivers could share their various stories about what was going on with them and whatever was actively bothering them. So, originally, I feel like this entire book should be Diane's story to tell and it is unbelievable to even me that I am the one writing a book like this, but dear reader, I am sure you have also done a few things in your life that makes you amazed.

Each day, after volunteering, she would come home to tell me how people were going through a lot even though she was not allowed to share the exact stories, except on their permission. So, all she did was come home and tell me about the various types of cancer and how going through chemotherapy was no child's play. Trust me, I didn't exactly listen much to her or hear all those terms, but with the knowledge of these things which I have now, going back in time, I understand everything a lot better and I can remember many of the things she used to tell me in the right context.

Diane always seemed burdened every time and sometimes, she stayed on the phone for long hours, saying she was having a one-on-one session with a caregiver. I wondered why anyone would get so worked up about another person's problem, but it was Diane. With her, it wasn't exactly very new. The support group she volunteered for made sure that each volunteer went through a six weeks course during which they learnt the right ways to talk to and counsel cancer patients in need of their help and response, both in person and on phone. I watched how helping patients became everything Diane cared about. She ate, watched TV and went for Sunday mass, but it all circled back to talking to patients and seeing how she could listen to help them. Even when she was not in the hospital, she would be on phone with them. Gradually, I began to admire her zeal, but I was sure that it would never be me to do such. I was not just the type. It was beautiful to watch, but I could not bring myself to be in those shoes. I was very sure that they would be too big for me.

I am a last born child and I am saying this to give you a large dose of perspective. I hate to admit it, but I have depended on people both directly and indirectly since when I knew my right from my left. So, having people depend on me to say words that would soothe them, or depend on me in any way at all is so scary. I don't want to imagine it. It's just too much responsibility and I do not think I can be equipped to handle such. At least, not yet. I like to say I am still a child, even though at the time Diane asked me to help, I was 18 years old, with an extra two months on it. I still see myself as a child as I am not ready to begin to handle adulthood responsibilities. However, I like to pop bottles the way adults do. Haha! Life is to be lived to the fullest. Well, Diane was 18 years old too quite alright, however, she had clocked 18 four months earlier than me, so you can't blame me much.

And please, don't ask me what happens when I become a mother. Trust me, when I get to that bridge, I would cross it. I just believe that everyone deserves to enjoy their youth to its fullest; nothing less.

Diane had volunteered for six months before asking me if I could step in and act in her place. I know she had planned to volunteer for a full year and work around preparing for any exam she had to take while volunteering. I think she got in and discovered that it was actually going to take more time and efforts than she had budgeted for and she could only be there the way she wanted to for the patients she worked with, only if she was fully invested. This is me just trying to relay my perception of the situation to you. Well, my perception in addition to what she ended up saying. Generally, I do not ask many question unless it is absolutely necessary. I make my decisions based on what I see, what a person willingly tells me and my perception of things. Maybe it is a bad habit, but this is something I have discovered about myself.

When Diane had said she wanted to discuss something with me earlier that day, I thought that my "perfect" and empathic cousin was carrying a baby. She had said the matter at hand was really important and as an eighteen-year-old who just finished high school and had seen a couple of our childhood friends get married or get pregnant, that was all I could think of. It was the kind of hot gist in town and everyone likes gist…I guess. The thought of being godmother was what made me remind her again about what she wanted to discuss with me. It wouldn't be bad at all to hear my cousin tell me that she and her amazing boyfriend were going to have a baby. They are both good looking, so I was looking at having a god-daughter that was definitely going to become a fashion model, or a god-son that was going to become a basketballer. It just had to be one of the two. Or maybe I was just thinking too far.

I live for such news…literally. So, you can imagine how disappointed I was when she told me that she was about to take the SATs and she wanted me to step into her shoes with the volunteer work. Her support group was short on volunteers at the time and she did not want the patients she was working with at the time, to suffer in any way.

I guess you're wondering what I was doing with my life at the time. Well, I'll tell you exactly what I was doing. I was not going to rush into anything like the others. I had a couple of interests; fashion, modeling or just pursuing a corporate career. I had always loved things like fashion and modeling since I was a kid. I am also book smart, even if I was not the very serious type in high school, so I could still work at having a corporate career. Honestly, it was hard to choose one at the point. Sometimes, those with multiple abilities are the real people that are faced with hard times in choosing a career path. Not flattering myself, but this was my case. So, I decided to just pause after high school and apply to go to college, fashion school or a modeling academy in the coming year. However, one thing was sure for me. I was not going to rush into anything in the moment. There was no reason for me to rush at all. I had everything I needed. Being the last child, asides my mom caring for Diane and me, I received lots and lots of gifts from my elder ones. They had made it their sole aim to make me happy since we lost our dad and I was the one that enjoyed only little of his fatherly affection. They truly wanted me to be happy, so I was at this stage of my life where I was under no pressure to do anything. My eldest brother was quite established and if I ever chose not to pursue any specific career, he had promised to establish a business for me. So, here I was, with many options and chilling till I could make the best decision for myself. Yeah, that's right—simply chilling. This is why Diane probably thought I was the best choice for the position. Maybe not the best best…more like, the most available choice. Yes, because I was literally chilling.

Anyway, when she told me that she needed me to step into her shoes as a volunteer, I laughed a lot. Who exactly did Diane think I was? I found the fact that she had decided to consider me an option to fit in for the kind of work she did. I was still trying to figure out my own life, how could I be helping anyone try to figure out theirs in the midst of their troubles too?

"You must be joking" I said. "You know, I just want to party this year and have serious moments in between to think about what I would like to do with my life."

Well, when I told you that I was taking the year off to think about what I would like to do with my future, I meant, I would spend a lot of time enjoying myself and avoiding being too serious altogether. I have heard countless times that adulthood is hard. I don't plan to take chances on enjoying while I can. There were many things I could not do as a high schooler when I had not clocked 18. Two months ago, I finally did and when I did, I knew it was time to enjoy my best life before the scary adulthood journey. You cannot blame me for thinking this way. If you have been an adult working and paying bills for a while, you would probably understand me better.

Hence, having Diane say I should dedicate all my time and throw aside all those plans that I had to enjoy my life now that I had turned 18 was just too crazy. How was that even supposed to work?

Now, let me refer you to my initial concerns about hospitals. Can you remember? Diane was basically asking me to leave my life that was planned out for fun and launch into a life that involved seeing sick people and hearing sad stories all day, every day. All these combined would be happening in a setting I did not like. It makes the whole thing a horrible idea.

"Please, many families will suffer if I pull out like this. The exams are drawing closer and I don't want to take chances at my SAT this time, so I need to devote enough time to preparation. You know I did not do so well in the previous year. Please, do this for me and all those sick people." Then, her demeanor changed. She held my shoulder as she stood across me, she smiled and said, "I believe you can do it." We both burst out into laughter at this point. That statement was too funny. I did not live to be serious; Diane knew this and I owned this fact too. The fact that I laughed however, did not mean that I had consented to the whole thing.

"I hear you girl. I hear you Diane. However, it's a big decision for me too. You know I have never liked the hospital setting. I mean, to work in that field will definitely be a blessing, but I do not just think I am wired for that, especially at this time."

"I get it." She said. "I did not mean to put you in such a tight position."

She said this, but Diane kept staring at me with a pitiful look, but I was not going to change my mind. She could see my resolve in my body language. She understood how I had always felt about the hospital setting, but I was too sure that she had no one else to turn to. Diane was never one to have many friends. She was the type of girl that was fine with having only two or three friends, and her two friends from high school had gotten admissions in other cities. They were the serious chaps in high school. Diane also got an admission immediately after high school, but it was not the school of her dreams. Hence, she wanted to take the SAT again and of course score high enough to get a place in the school of her dreams. The point I am trying to make here is that she had no other friend to ask for this favor. The only other friends she had made were from the support group and their hands were full as well. She had said this previously. So I knew that there was literally nothing they could do to help. I was her only option. However, she had always known about my issues with working in a hospital. So, she did not push.

The fact that she did not push also made me begin to give it a second thought. What if I could adjust to that setting? I was a rebel. If you push for me to do something, I am more likely not to do it than if you leave me to decide on my terms. I guess she had come to know the kind of person I was.

But, probably not. I slept over it and I even tried to watch some movies about surgeries, just to see if I could possibly cope with that setting. First off, Diane is not one to ask for favors, so I knew she really needed this. Well, that is on one hand. On the other hand, I thought about the fact that families might actually suffer, not having someone to talk to, someone like Diane. Now, that was another issue. Diane was the diligent one. I have always been the relaxed and a bit spoilt one, but maybe I could learn. However, I lived with Diane; she could put me through and perhaps, I could dedicate time to learning about cancer and how I could come in as a volunteer to help too. And oh! There's that six weeks training course she took that was directed at helping her to actually help people in the oncology unit where she worked. If I could have that, perhaps I would measure up too. I may not be as perfect as Diane was, but at least, I would fill in for the time being. More volunteers may just join, who knows? And then, I would opt out and be free to live on my terms yet again.

I realized I was already thinking of how to help and how I could measure up to the standards Diane had set. Hence, it dawned on me that there was a chance that I could adjust. However, I did not want to give Diane an answer right away. First, that would be too easy for her. Haha! Of course, I am the type to make people wait and work for things—my ex from high school can you tell you several tales. Secondly, I wanted to actually think things through properly before giving her an answer. I was not one to put my hands into a course and then take my hands off it when the going gets tough. I choose if I really want to do something, and then, I stick to it to the very end. However, in this case, I thought there was a chance that I would bolt on this one if there were other people to fill up the position. Either way, since it was all subject to chance, I still had to think properly.

So, I started doing my research before giving Diane any feedback at all. So, I started from the very scratch by trying to know what cancers really mean. Don't worry, I'm not going to bore you in any way. I just want you to know every detail of my discoveries as I take you on my journey.

So, when you hear "cancer", this is what should come to your mind: a group of diseases (as there are many forms of cancers) in which cells grow abnormally. Now, these cells that grow abnormally now have the ability to extend themselves to other parts of the body. It is also essential for you to know that cancers are commonly called malignant tumors. However, when you hear benign tumors, those ones do not spread to any other part of the body. So, benign tumors are not associated with cancer. Hence, it is safe to say that not every tumor is a cancer.

I hope that was simple enough. Read it again. Well, that's the interpretation of my discovery about cancer.

Now, I have heard Diane talk about working in the oncology unit so many times. So, what happens in the oncology unit of a hospital? The oncology or chemotherapy unit is the area of the hospital where patients going through chemotherapy treatment for cancer. Many of the patients are usually on admission in that unit of the hospital, depending on the type and the stage of their cancer. Some others come for treatment over there and go home too, based on how severe their cancer has become. I began to watch videos of patients in the oncology unit of some hospitals online and this made me see how many of these patients were literally struggling for their lives on those hospital beds. Many were on various types of support because of the side effects of chemotherapy. Yet, they had to take the treatment, because it was how their cancers got better and how they stayed alive.

It would surprise you to know of the various kinds of cancer that exist. The numbers surprised me even more, as I realized that over two hundred types of cancers have been identified and researched. They are basically named by the organs or the tissues from which the cancer stems. So, when you hear of "breast cancer", it is found in the breast tissue, skin cancer; in the skin and the list goes on and on. The cancers you will commonly hear about include breast cancer, prostate cancer, bladder cancer, lung cancer, colorectal cancer, skin cancer (also called melanoma), kidney cancer, non-Hodgkin lymphoma, thyroid cancer, leukemia, pancreatic cancer, endometrial cancer, and liver cancer. Reading through the list and what happens in each type of cancer hurt me a lot, because it felt like having a part of your body you love or need to function betray you. It basically betrays you by producing cells that are harmful. The cells in that part of your body don't stop at that. They also go on to spread to other parts of your body that are totally innocent in this equation. How annoying can anything be? It is just like having a bad egg among your close friends, who does not stop at talking silly about you, but taking that talk to other important friends of yours and ruining all those friendships till you have no one to run to when you are in trouble. Just think of that. That's what cancer does, spreading into innocent parts of your body until even vital organs are affected. I know that description was too detailed; well, I have been there before. I have had such a friend and now, I know how to identify those from miles afar and avoid them. However, as for cancer, most people don't see it coming and as for avoiding it, research is still ongoing as cancers are relatively new to the world.

The worst part is that you can try your best to cut down on the risk of having some of these cancers. Skin cancers for instance, you can avoid bleaching. For lung cancers, you can avoid smoking. However, these things only largely reduce the risk for having the cancers. It does not entirely exempt you from having these cancers. Sometimes, heredity plays a huge role, as seen in prostate cancer and in fact, in all types of cancer. You know, I never really understand why just being born into a particular family or by a particular person sets you up to have a condition that eventually leads to a person's death. It is so annoying to even think of the fact that this is some people's reality. For people like that, I keep wondering; what's the point of being born? To suffer? I have tried hard to make sense of this and here, I am not even referring to sickle cell patients and parents who knew they risked having a child with the condition by getting together. That's an entirely different ball game.

I can only imagine what people living with cancer of any type go through. My granny died of a certain cancer, but I would talk about that much later. Even while looking at cancer patients go through all that pain, all you can really do is imagine. Many a time, it is not their fault. And even if it is their fault, the kind of suffering and pain I saw in those videos I watched made me wonder if anyone deserved to suffer like that even if they ever did anything to bring such situations to themselves. These people have to go through a treatment that is supposed to help them heal, but also makes them suffer—chemotherapy. No, nobody deserves that. That was my own resolution that night, as I closed all the tabs on my laptop, in my preparation to go to bed.

I knew that I had made up my mind to be a source of encouragement to the helpless. Watching those videos alone, I could feel their pain. There were literally helpless. I wondered how their family members felt. Imagine looking at a loved one suffer, but not being able to help them at all.

I knew that at this point, my response to Diane would be a positive one. Not just because she asked me, but because I had come to the point in my mind where I could put my hate for the hospital environment away and focus on something that really mattered—helping the next person in my own little way. I would be playing a part in helping with what people of the noble medical profession did. Additionally, I had made her wait for an answer for about eight days. She had earned this response of mine by the virtue of waiting patiently. Mind you, I'm not even petty.

"Thank you! Thank you!! Thank you!!!" Diane kept saying as she kept hugging me.

"Take it easy on me girl." I said. Well, I am not particularly a hugger and I am definitely not one to throw my feelings around. I liked the fact that she was hugging me like that, but I was not going to show her that. She knew me too well; it was not surprising to her that I acted like I did not care. She knew that my head was in fact swelling at the fact that she appreciated my response that much.

"When you are done hugging me, would you please tell me if I would also go through the six weeks training?"

"Of course, you would go through that to equip you for volunteering. I mean, do you even know what to say or how to act around someone who is grieving?"

"I'm certified girl."

We laughed. I was glad that I was going to have that training. Of course, I needed it.

"Hold on! Does that mean I would register newly; not like I'm merely covering for an already registered member?"

"Well, you have to register as a new member." Diane said, drawing back from me because she knew I would react with my scream. But I chose to disappoint her this time. I was now an adult. I have now chosen to only act like one at all times, and that meant not screaming at things like that as I used to do in the past.

"I would need another 24 hours to think about that. I did not have this information before now Diane. You did not explain to me. I thought you only wanted me to cover for you." Frankly, I felt like she wanted to pull me into the support group in a cunning way, but I was not sure, so I did not want to accuse her just like that. Diane is a very straightforward person. Perhaps if it was someone else, I would have come up with my accusation very easily. I had no issue with signing up as a new volunteer. I just hate being forced or manipulated to commit to anything. I like to think things through and have the pride that I made the decision by myself.

"I'm really sorry girl. You know your response was not quite on the positive side the first time I brought up the issue. So, I did not think to go any further with the details. I had to wait to get even the slightest greenlight from you, but you decided to take me by surprise even with your positive response."

Innocent as ever. Just as innocent as I thought she would be. "Alright b."

The following week, Diane began to prepare for her SATs and as for me, I went to register as a volunteer. If someone had told me two weeks before then that I would register to volunteer in a hospital setting, I would have called such a person a big joke, because no…it did not work like that. People did not experience life-changing circumstances just like that. It wouldn't have made any sense to me at all. But here I was, volunteering for Helping hands support group, all smiles.

The six weeks of training began and it was quite an interesting one. We were thought about body languages and how people interpreted them. We were also thought how to apply them in relating to the patients as well as their caregivers. We learnt a whole lot of skills I never imagined I would be learning. Anything could happen and we would be the only ones around to give CPR to anyone. We learnt that. We learnt basic transfer skills too; how to move patients in different situations. We were trained by professionals and given certifications for some of these skills after practicing. This way, we were actually authorized to do these things, but only in situations were no medical personnel was present of course. I made sure to put my heart to each skill and the entire learning process, as I had seen how much those patients suffer and the burden on their caregivers in those videos. With each passing day, I surprised myself by getting even more dedicated. I really wanted to help as much as I could. I did not want to contribute to their problems by doing anything wrongly. Each day, I got home to see Diane studying and I found myself discussing everything I had learnt with her, showing so much excitement while at it. I also discussed all my fears with her and she kept reminding me that those fears were very valid. I just had to keep applying myself to the process. On some nights, we discussed all through and then, bonded over movies. We would sleep into late hours of the morning, but thankfully, my training started by 12 noon every day and she had the entire day to study once I left.

Whenever I got to the support group center, I made sure to mind my business all the time. Not like it was planned; it just came naturally to me. As much as I like to talk and I am especially free with those that are truly close to me, I also keep my distance from those that are not close to me and I am usually quiet around them too. As for new people, I hardly go all out to make new friends. If somehow life brings us together, great. If life does not bring us together, then I would stop at greetings and nothing more than that. That's just me.

The process got more interesting with each passing week and I also became more interested and invested. If you ever saw me with those materials from the training, you would dare to think that I had an exam to write, but I didn't. There were bonding sessions too and that was how I started talking to Fiona.

By the fourth week, our facilitator asked us to pick a partner for make-believe counselling. That we did. I turned to my side and I saw this pretty brunette. She said her name was Fiona and then we started our make-believe counselling session. We exchanged roles with each round; sometimes, I was the counsellor, at other times, she was the counsellor. We found ourselves laughing a lot during the sessions because we were making lots and lots of mistakes. While we made those mistakes, it was somewhat fun too. Fiona had a good vibe. She sort of made learning fun for me. It was our fourth week and I think our natures were somewhat similar because she was yet to make any friend too. She was apparently calm and reserved. Thanks to my nature, I had not seen her around, while she admitted to seeing me around severally.

Throughout that week, we stayed back when other left to practice our roles better. We had the common desire to actually know what to do when people that needed help presented themselves. For this reason, we bonded quite well. I must mention that I did not know that this was the kind of friendship I needed. I mean, mum was always away for work and Diane was always too busy with her preparation for SATs. She was also taking some online tutorials to brace up. Hence, she hardly ever had time to hang out. After our time at the support group center, Fiona was that friend that would suggest that we went for ice cream. I had missed that I did not even realize it until Fiona showed up. It was always like that with my friends from high school and my ex too. However, you know how life tends to scatter up people. I could say that happened with my clique from high school. So, I had been stuck with Diane for months and I did not even know what it felt like to have fun in a spontaneous way like that.

Well, I was committed to enjoying this ride. The more I got to know Fiona, the more I realized that she was just my perfect kind of friend. She was indeed my ideal kind of friend. Now, I had my freedom and this friendship—pure bliss!

In my short period of existence in this world, I have learnt a whole lot of things; from my friends, from my mum. In fact, the list of people I have learnt from is an endless one. I have also learnt from my experiences and trust me, there are quite a number of them—good and bad. Hence, I can say I know a lot of things about life. I also have hopes and plans on how my life should probably play out. However, I did not see what I am about to tell you in the entirety of this book coming. I never imagined that I would be in a hospital setting, working to help anyone at all and I certainly did not know that taking this step and being a volunteer would change my life forever. I did not know that the way I think, the way I view things and my whole perspective about life was about to change. Perhaps, this shift in my thinking was because I was now standing in a different place. Whenever you change the position of your stance, your view is sure to change and this is exactly what happened to me.

Life is quite unpredictable. The best we can do is hope, plan and pray; the future we want might even manifest in a way we never imagined. I am in a very different place than where I was when I started volunteering. Meeting people going through things you never imagined probably did that to me. Many of us grow up in controlled settings—controlled by our parents, controlled by our loved ones. They shield us from whatever they think would hurt us and when we dare to imagine that some things would go a certain way that is termed negative or that the odds would not be in our favor, they tell us to dismiss that kind of things. While it is true that we are the architect of our destinies, the truth is that life happens. I guess this is the case because we cannot control what we go through in the course of having our dreams become our reality. It is funny how cancer made me begin to see things differently; I never imagined this would be the case for me.

However, meeting some kinds of people made me discover an aspect of life I did not know about. Meeting people who equally hoped for the best but ended up having to take care of a partner or a parent with cancer for a long time made me think very differently. It made me realize that life is indeed no bed of roses for many and if you have it great on your side, live in the moment and enjoy it all to the fullest. On this journey I never expected that I would embark, I have cried, I have laughed, I have seen people celebrate victories and also cry at the realization of defeat and hopelessness.

I am about to show you so much about cancer that you did not know. There are so many sides to cancer that people do not know. There are so many stories that have not been told. The importance of these stories is that they would help people in getting the right idea about cancer and provide them with the strength to face the challenges that would present; after being pre-informed by the stories of other people. The caregivers are usually very pre-occupied in every possible way; physically, emotionally and mentally, up to the point that they do not have the time to encourage someone going through a similar situation. They are usually drained. Hence, let's say I would serve as the middleman that gives you information by bringing you into what was my world, during the one year I volunteered in the oncology unit of a hospital. Of course, all these stories were told with the permission of the patients (where they could) and/or their next of kin.

If you have a relative with cancer of you've been diagnosed with it yourself, then you should definitely keep reading this book. It was written to open the eyes of everyone to the different journeys people embark on once they have the condition; maybe on a surface level because I have never had cancer myself. However, I can tell you what I have seen and noticed firsthand. You would see the realities of many people with different types of cancer, but you would also be encouraged when you see their coping strategies and the recovery process of some. For me, my one year of being a volunteer was no walk in the park. It was a journey that was quite emotionally draining. However, I would forever be grateful for that same journey. Looking back, I do not regret being a volunteer one bit. Come with me on this journey; one that changed my life forever.

CHAPTER TWO

alking into Desire's ward has to be the most heartbreaking thing I have ever experienced. I had been talking on phone with her sister, Mandy, who is about my age for a while and encouraging her, but I finally got to enter Desire's ward. I don't mean that the condition of things in there was heartbreaking. I mean, it was quite obvious that her parents had given her the highest level of comfort possible by placing her in that cozy room in St. Greg's. So, I am not referring to her living conditions (in terms of provision) as heartbreaking. It was just the realization of all Mandy had been telling me on phone; the reality of Desire going through that much pain and retrogression in terms of development. Again, it was so heartbreaking to see this.

There were pictures of the girl doing great things; winning the spelling bee competition for her school's district and collecting several awards for her age category. It was apparent that she was a bright kid. She was a star that had only just begun to shine. There was also another big portrait of her receiving an award for being the best-behaved kid in her class. There were several pictures of her classmates holding placards that said, 'get well soon' at various positions in her room. She was a pretty girl aged 10 years old. Everything in her room seemed perfect and neatly arranged; her pink teddy bear was in a corner and the way the portraits were carefully arranged all over the place. It was obvious that her parents were trying to give her the highest level of comfort and has Mandy said on the phone, they were working extra hours and taking extra shifts to achieve that.

There were encouraging quotes all over the place and everything indeed seemed in order; except for the health of the young girl. Her eyes; they were so innocent, as she laid there, with the drip being administered into her veins and the huge pipe passed in through her chest to administer treatment. She had her hair wrapped and although she seemed to try to make her face come alive, there was little she could do.

She was the first real patient I was visiting and to be honest, I had developed cold feet. The stories her sister had told me about the girl and what I was seeing now was contributing to how much I felt like nothing I was ever going to say was going to be enough to explain how such an innocent girl would be suffering from leukemia. Everything I had learnt flew out of my head at the point. I was just drowned in the ocean of pity and the feeling that there was almost nothing I could say to make them feel better or I wish I just knew what I could say at the point.

"Hello Gabby." Said Mandy to me, seeming excited to see me. I just stood there with my thoughts coming together that these people actually feel like there is something I would say that would make them feel better. But I was wrong. Sometimes, all you have to do is listen with care.

"It's nice to finally have you here." Mandy continued.

At this point, I remembered what Diane told me. A tip that had always helped her was to smile, "but briefly" she had said. She explained to me how these people were going through a lot already and just having someone smile can light up the whole room. The family of the patient may not have many reasons to smile on some days, but as a volunteer, you could come in smiling and literally make their day. You could be the light they need in a room. At the training, we learnt that it may feel wrong to smile because of their situation, but they already know what it is. They already know the situation they're in and the last thing they want is pity. This is why many people going through things prefer to keep it all to themselves until they have overcome that situation, because nobody really wants pity out of anything. Acquaintances are always guilty of offering pity, so they'd rather not tell them anything about how they feel. Patients and caregivers just want sincere concern, but not pity. So, back to the trick Diane was trying to teach me: smile but briefly, probably while saying your greetings. Then, get back to sincerely caring about their needs and how you could help in the moment.

The aim of everything you are set to do is to show empathy and not sympathy. You might be wondering why I am even bothered about a caregiver like Mandy, or why I would be concerned about caregivers in general. Isn't the concern always the cancer patient?

Well, to answer that: I am bothered about caregivers and of course the patient too, but caregivers in particular because the patient may not be in the position to respond or even discuss how they feel many a time, but caregivers are the ones that can directly reach out to the patient and reaching out to the patient in a great way would only happen if the state of their own mind is great.

"Hey Mandy!" I smiled, as I hugged her. I was sincerely excited to meet her too, as I had found a friend in her. "It's nice to finally see you in person, and how are you doing today?" I asked.

"Oh well, I am alright. A few running around to do as always, but it is for the best."

"Yes, it is definitely for the best." I said.

"And how's Desire today?"

"Oh, she's alright."

"You've been here alone, taking care of her."

"No, my mom just left. She had been here all day, since she was off work today. She had to go home to make dinner, so she could bring some here."

"Dinner sounds great. Sounds like someone has her appetite back." I said this because over the phone, Mandy had mentioned how she had lost her appetite earlier on as her as her sister's blood count kept dropping as a negative response to chemotherapy. Now, she seemed happy at the mention of dinner.

"Oh yes! Her blood count is a lot better now. My appetite is back." No one really talks about the attachment care givers end up having with family members with cancer. This is not surprising as everything that happens in the family revolves around their care and the whole attachment thing begins subconsciously.

"So, hope you've not been bored in here. I see Desire is sleeping."

"Oh yes. She's sleeping soundly. I have been playing some games on my phone."

"Oh…let me see!" I said excitedly.

"Sure."

We took turns at playing the games and cheered each other on. I loved how her face was lit up the whole period. We even thought about having a board game (like chess or monopoly) that we could have there in the hospital and play quietly when we were alone. Then all of a sudden, she paused and I was sure that Mandy was going to let out a serious thought. It was one of those moments.

"You know, my family has to be very careful because of the things can subject my sister to infections. It is crazy, but we have to think properly about the kind of public places we would like to eat if we want to eat out. We have to be extra careful about anything and everything because we do not want to do anything that hurts her. I guess my family is just a bit weird. The doctors said even though she does not live at home for now, we have to get used to living like that, so by the time she comes home, we'll already be used to it."

"No! Your family is not weird. You are a strong family, with members that are not afraid to guard a member in the best way they can. It takes a great deal of love to do that and that love is lacking in our world. You have it, so that sets you apart."

"Gabby, you don't get it. I have lost friends and my parents have lost friends too. All these have happened because they did not understand why my family is the way it is. I guess they don't just understand leukemia, but instead of trying to learn, they act out of their own ignorance and just stay away."

"You got it just right. They are ignorant and you are not to be blamed for that. Look, no matter how bad things go in life, those that are for you would definitely find their way to you."

"That's true. You are an evidence of the fact that this is correct. Look at you, once a stranger, but right here, cheering me on. I wish my parents were just here to see you, to meet you."

"That would have been great, but we're having fun anyway."

"Yes, we are. I still can't wait for you to meet them."

The evening ended with us going through the life book that their parents had made for Desire. It included the good days when she used to win trophies and all that. It also included the time of her transition into her illness. It included Desire's moments of laughter even in the course of the illness and the times she crossed a major milestone (an instance was her first chemotherapy treatment session). Mandy teared up as she looked through. It was tears of joy about how far they had come from the first time she was diagnosed and the entire family of five was in despair. There was a third child; their younger brother and he was doing his own little quota in cooperating with his parents and his elder sister by being so well-behaved while they did a good job at caring for Desire.

I started talking to Mandy on phone a while ago. I talked to her and realized that she was very much like me. She liked to go out and party. In high school, she was one of the cool kids. She is definitely the kind of friend I would love to have. Talking with her over the phone just made me see that she was no different from me. Her family had just started experiencing a new situation and she needed a friend to talk to outside her circle. So, she was more than happy when she realized I was the new volunteer counsellor. Many of the families already spend a lot on treatment, so having counselling sessions would cost even more.

For most of them, having a volunteer counsellor from a support group like ours was a blessing and they certainly did not take that for granted. Helping Hands had been in existence for quite a while, so my support group was quite popular in the oncology unit and on the wards of St. Greg's; and in fact, the entire city.

Mandy did not seem to have connected with Diane a lot. She told me this after a few days of talking. First off, she was reluctant to talk to me about how she really felt about the whole situation. However, later on, when she started talking more, she told me that she liked my vibe and she had no issue opening up to me because she felt I was a friend. And that was the reason why she was telling me that much at all. I had also begun to see her as my friend. It was not strange that we talked long hours on the phone every single day.

Diane now made fun of me. I was now doing what she used to do and I would mock her for. However, she was proud still. Honestly, I felt sort of uncool for doing what Diane used to do, but I was enjoying it. I can't deny that because I would be lying. I like how involved I have gotten with Mandy and how I had been able to help in my own little way. She also made me feel cool. She didn't make me feel like I was doing stuff for uncool kids. Yes, I still worried about things like that at the time. What did you expect? I am teenager. Sorry, not sorry.

She had warmed up to me a lot. She was able to tell me about the things that bothered her and her joys. Yes, her joys. There are joys recorded even in the midst of her troubles. She was very happy that the situation, as bad as it was had made her family bond in ways they could never imagine.

Ever thought of those friends who you regularly got in trouble often with in high school or middle school? Those are the kinds of friends that if you run into in three to five years, you would always feel like you have a strong bond because you passed through trying times together. That is the way I could relay what she explained to me. That was how she and the members of her family now felt; strengthened and bonded through an adversity.

"Once upon a time, you know, as a teenager, I used to have a lot of arguments with my parents, but now, we all have a common goal of rooting for Desire and that creates such a strong connection between us all. We have to talk about many difficult issues with respect to my sister's health, so right now, we just have each other's back. I do not know anything else that we have had to deal with that was this difficult, so it's all good." Mandy said. "Right now, we hardly have fights and we all relate as friends. I can literally talk to them about anything now and since we see each other as real friends, I can say for sure that they would not judge me."

She also talked about how her kid brother, Liam was more well-behaved than a child his age would typically be. He was doing so well in school and giving no one any cause to worry thanks to the basic understanding of what was going on in the family. She was grateful for that. She never imagined a time like that would come for her family, so she felt blessed; talk about finding a source of light in a tunnel. She was also ever grateful for the amazing staff at St. Greg's and how they were quite helpful in making things easier for her family. The treatment of the leukemia was complicated enough and they have to check the change in her blood count from time to time.

"The staff here are so patient. They explain all procedures to us thoroughly and answer as many questions as we ask." Said Mandy. She went on and on about the things she was grateful for and it was then I understood why she had some sort of peace. When we express gratitude even in the most difficult situations, then it becomes somewhat easier to see the light at the end of the tunnel. Mandy could see the light. Yet, this did not mean she was in denial of her struggles.

Mandy wanted to go to college so much, but her family really needed her at the time. She had gotten an admission at the time her sister was diagnosed (some months back), but she had to defer to the following year. It was a huge sacrifice, but it had to be made. They could not also begin to think of the extra costs that was sure to come with at the moment. Also, there was the part of the additional support she provided that was very much needed in the home at the time. She wanted to go to college so bad. However, she did not need a lesson about if now was the best time to discuss her concerns with her parents. It was certainly not a good time and she was not going to push it.

Discussing with Mandy was definitely making my immature self a bit more grown in my thinking. The situation was making her take responsibility like those of her age probably cannot. I absolutely loved to see it, because it made me wonder if I would be able to do the same in her position. She also challenged me to want to be better at putting the urgent needs of those I loved over my own more superficial wants. I loved and respected my new friend, Mandy, even more.

While you must be familiar with the fact that Desire is suffering from Leukemia by now, you may be wondering what the term really means and what it connotes for the child. Well, I had to read up about it myself and I would now explain everything I have learnt over here. Now, let's get a little insight into what is going on in Desire's body and why her family has to stand behind her solidly the way they are doing.

Leukemia basically means 'cancer of the blood'. As with every cancer, there are cancer cells and here, they grow in the bone marrow. The bone marrow is a tissue. It is spongy and it is found inside the bones. The cells in the bone marrow are what go on to form red blood cells, white blood cells and platelets, which are essentially the components of the blood. When a child (as in Desire's case) has leukemia, the cells made by the bone marrow are abnormal in the sense that they do not mature. In this case, the abnormal cells are usually the white blood cells (the very cells that were designed to fight infections). The bone marrow also makes a few healthy cells, but the abnormal cells develop faster. They work a lot rapidly than the healthy cells.

So, essentially, the cancer cells grow in the bone and you know the bad part about cancers. As discussed earlier, the abnormal cells would move from there into other parts of the body. In this case, the rapidly developing cancer cells moves from the bone marrow into the blood.

Let me tell you a bit more about Leukemia. There are different types of it in children. However, most of the time, the leukemia seen in children is always the acute type, especially as that is the case for Desire. Some of the types are the Acute lymphocytic leukemia (ALL), Acute myelogenous leukemia (AML), Chronic myelogenous leukemia (CML), chronic lymphocytic leukemia (CLL), Juvenile myelomonocytic leukemia (JMML) and Hybrid or mixed lineage leukemia. Desire had the Acute lymphocytic leukemia (ALL) which is actually the most common of them all.

While you may be wondering why any child would have their life come to a halt (at least for a while) because of this sad turn of events, let me quickly tell you that there is no exact known cause of leukemia in kids, just like every other type of cancer where there's hardly ever a known cause. However, childhood leukemia is not hereditary, but certain other conditions that make a child have the childhood leukemia can be inherited from their parents.

It has been traced by researchers that there are usually mutations (changes) in the genes of the bone marrow cells that lead to this condition in kids. These changes can happen spontaneously, in the early life of the child or possibly before the child is even born.

A child who is usually exposed to high level of radiation (which could be from all sorts of technological devices), has inherited a condition which affects the body's immune system, has inherited a syndrome (e.g Li-Fraumeni Syndrome and Down's syndrome) or has a sibling with leukemia stands a chance of having the condition.

Remember that these cancer cells enter the blood. For this reason, it is very easy to have it spread to various tissues and organs. The spread can be to very strategic organs or tissues in the body like the liver, thymus, spinal cord, brain, lymph nodes and spleen.

The symptoms vary for each child and can include tiredness, headaches, pale skin, dizziness, fever, difficulty in breathing, fever, long-term infections, bruising and bleeding (e.g in the gums), abdominal swelling, weight loss, pain in the bones or joints, poor appetite, swollen lymph nodes. Not all these can be seen in a child, but a range of it could occur. Now, imagine a child going through multiple of these symptoms, how hard it must be for the child to live. The worst part is the fact that the condition can look like any other health condition and each symptom on its own could mean something different. A child going through any of these certainly needs to see a health care professional as soon as possible.

She had the Acute lymphocytic leukemia (ALL) and hers was the common ALL (B-cell staging). The staging of acute lymphocytic leukemia is different from that of other cancers which have their staging described in terms of numbers. She was receiving intensive chemotherapy gradually, as she was going to receive it long-term. She had to be in the hospital for the initial stage for months before she would be able to start coming in as an outpatient to the oncology unit of St. Greg's hospital. The induction stage of her chemo was directed at taking care of the cancer cells that her spread into her brain and spinal cord. The cells had been discovered by doing a lumbar puncture that revealed so.

All the various treatments and how the body of the 10-year-old was being assessed and treated was taking an emotional toll on her family too. She was too young for all that trouble, yet it was for the best.

It was about 11a.m in St. Greg's Hospital and meeting Mrs. Green, Desire's mother that morning definitely hit different. It was different from meeting my friend Mandy as usual, but the warm and cheerful nature of Mrs. Green was quite encouraging.

"I have heard so much about you from Mandy. She speaks highly of you."

"Oh! I'm sure she didn't have much to say."

"Haha! I am not surprised. She already told me how humble you are."

At this point, I was speechless. Mandy had called me that morning. Mrs. Green just needed an outlet. She was going through a lot with multi-tasking at running the home, working her job and the burden of care of their daughter. She just wanted to talk to someone different and that was why a support group like ours was created. She had asked Mandy to call me up and I was more than happy to show up. I was glad that I was doing something that was indeed relevant. When I used to watch Diane go to St. Greg's, I used to wonder if she was really making any impact. I mean, healthcare professionals were already there to take care of patients. What exactly was a volunteer like me supposed to do? On a subconscious level, I always felt like people who volunteer do so to feel better about themselves. I mean, everyone likes to feel like they are doing something important, but how relevant was volunteering really when healthcare workers were there? It was harsh to ever think that, but if you see me in the light of a spoilt last born kid, then you would not see me as mean for saying those kinds of things—just spoilt. Well, this was how I used to think; not anymore.

During my six weeks of training, I began to see the relevance of volunteering, but not the way I saw it on this particular morning. Mrs. Green had really wanted to speak to someone who was not exactly working in the hospital. This confirmed the role of volunteers in providing a vital means of complementing the healthcare team by attending to the non-medical needs of patients, hence making the patient's experience better. When this role is properly understood, the synergy makes everything better for the patients.

Mrs. Green looked like she had a lot to say. Mandy had to go back to the house to pick up some things and Mr. Green who had a white collar job was at work.

"Watching your child suffer this way is no fun, Trust me." She started. "Seeing a child you carried for so long and nursed for ten years go sick all of a sudden brings a lot of pain that probably cannot be explained."

She paused.

"I'm sorry Gabby. I have a lot to say and Mandy speaks highly of you..."

"Ma'am, it is okay to talk."

"Thanks. I am just used to support groups. You know, they've been so helpful since all these started. I mean, it's only been four months into this, but I have experienced help from your support group. The meetings and of course the amazing representatives that are usually assigned to us."

"I understand you ma'am."

There was a long pause between us and I knew enough to let her have things her way and start talking once she was ready.

"Seeing a child you nursed grow up and begin to move through the various stages of development is beautiful. You know, seeing your child sit, crawl, walk with support and somehow find their way to begin to actually walk. It's amazing! It brings so much joy to the heart of anyone that has birthed a child. But…"

"Can you just imagine what it feels like, not only to have the child stop growing, but also for that child to start losing all those skills and movement ways they had learnt? Can you imagine what it feels like to see your child progress five steps forward and after celebrating, watch that child go back to zero and then some more."

She paused before she continued. "I felt like my world was crashing down when Desire suddenly became different. She was not just a child that was crawling or merely walking. She was a smart child who had accrued several great things, but all of a sudden, when she lost her ability to walk, she also began to lose her smartness gradually. I'm sure you saw all she has participated in and the awards she had won even as a child. She had such zeal. She was brilliant and also courageous. So, you can imagine how hard it was to watch a child like her change like that, but I was there all along, I saw her go from bad to worse and felt helpless. All I could do was bring her up to the hospital anytime she was sick or experienced a different change."

"You did your best as a mother ma'am. No one prepares anyone to face something like this." Mrs. Green heaved a sigh and continued saying her story.

Following this, all Desire could do was crawl again. Yet, while crawling, she did it like her feet was hurting. Of course, Mrs. Green mentioned how they got her a wheel chair to move her around, but they wanted her to move to some extent, as it had been advised by the doctors, since they hadn't discovered what it was and they did not want her joints to get stiffened. That was the reason they let her crawl.

"All the while, we were visiting the closest hospital close to our home and they could not exactly find out what was going on with my child. All we could do was manage the symptoms while many tests were being run on her. She stopped schooling for the time being, but it meant nothing because you know, when troubles come, your priorities change. There was a time she spontaneously started walking again, and then, she went back to not being able to work. Like you said, no one prepares anyone for this and even more, the rollercoaster of emotions that come with things like this. With every movement she made, every joint in her body ached and it was not hard to see."

At this point, tears were rolling down her cheeks and I tried to hand her a handkerchief, but she won't even let me. She gestured for me to just sit where I sat and do nothing. I respected that.

She wiped her tears with her palm and continued. "You know, we all wondered if something happened at school, but Desire had always been a vocal and assertive child, she would have spoken up if there was anything like that. We also asked at her school and even went through all the surveillance cameras to see if there was anything suspicious that had happened. We found absolutely nothing. She had gone about her normal activities like every normal kid."

Very soon, the complaint shifted to her running a high fever every night. They went back to their family pediatrician who had been monitoring her all the while. The hospital was the closest to their house and there had been several tests here and there. They also ran x-rays and tests which came out negative. No one really wakes up and suspects their child has cancer, so I do not blame even the pediatrician. From the little I know, doctors like to rule out all simpler possible causes of symptoms before calling the bigger names. That's just how it worked. The pains in the joints were suspected to be from rheumatoid arthritis. Hence, they were referred to the rheumatologist. All tests and scans were negative for rheumatoid arthritis. So, further investigation just had to be done.

Hence, she was referred to St. Greg's as it was renown in their city for solving complex cases. The rheumatologist had suggested that Desire needed to see a hematologist. It was suspected that whatever was causing that much pain may have to do with her blood.

"We visited St. Greg's hospital the next day and my baby was diagnosed with acute lymphocytic leukemia (ALL) after they performed a biopsy of her bone marrow and seeing that there were leukemia cells in her bone marrow."

On hearing cancer, the entire family was devastated. Even little Liam knew that something was wrong. He knew his sister had been sick all the while, but the family had never been as sad as they were in that moment it was confirmed to be cancer, so he knew that there was surely more to it. At that point, Mr. & Mrs. Green as well as Mandy knew they would have to commit to family in a way they had never done. No matter the extent of the cancer, it always took a lot whenever a member of a family had cancer of any type. At least, that was sure from the little they knew about cancers.

"The moment they mentioned the diagnosis, my heart was definitely broken." Said Mrs. Green. The look in her eye gave me an insight into how it felt on that day.

Luckily, the disease is quite a treatable one. The prognosis was quite good. It relieved the family a bit to hear that, but it did not mean the condition would disappear all at once.

Just the way you see Desire each time you walk into her room in the oncology unit, they put a port through her chest so she could receive chemotherapy. After a while, once she had gotten better and her pain was somewhat reduced, a physical therapist began to coach Desire on how to walk again. A long trip had begun for the Greens, one that was sure to have a mix of fears and victories; as expected in the journey that is cancer treatment. She had been on admission for five months and the entire treatment was supposed to take two to three years, depending on how she responded to treatment.

One of the issues Mandy discussed with me that especially bothered her each time she thought about going to college was the fact that health insurance did not cover for all the tests and treatments her sister needed to do. Yet, her parents wanted her sister to have the most comfortable recovery phase possible. Hence, they were pumping all the money they had into caring for her. There was so much to spend on and she knew her parents were drained. It cannot be denied by anyone who has ever had a cancer patient in their family that the expenses never really finish. Life-saving cancer therapy is expensive. Hospitalization alone and the cost for thing you just never saw coming strains the account of the affected family. Mrs. Green tried to take on more shifts, but whenever there was a change in Desire's health circumstances, she had to drop those shifts and be around for her child. As far as the Greens were concerned, in spite of how Mandy acted, she was still very much a child to them and they were not going to place the entire burden of caring on her sister on her because it was just too much for anyone to handle at a young age.

"Mandy just started out adulthood and trust me, it gets even more stressful and draining with time. I mean, adulthood comes with a lot of freedom, but there is also the responsibility of taking care of your own troubles. I don't want to stress my little girl out before she even begins to deal with her own problems."

The way a mother loves a child cannot be compared to any other love. Mandy had begun to feel like her parents were not showing her enough love. Whereas, here was her mom telling me how she was thinking of Mandy's future and how she did not want the responsibilities they were giving her to affect her adulthood.

"I am sure Mandy would love to hear things like these from you. I'm sure she would want to hear that you care about her too."

I love Mrs. Green's reaction. She just nodded, but I could tell that she understood exactly what I was saying. She understood that Mandy had somewhat been feeling neglected, but had to probably tuck in how she felt because of what currently mattered to the family.

Mandy returned and Mrs. Green went to give her a hug.

"You know I love you, right?"

Mandy just looked down. She hadn't felt loved all along.

"I love you my darling daughter and I am grateful for all the sacrifices you have made for the family. I just want you to know that I see them. Your father and I talk about them and we really appreciate everything you do. Mandy said nothing; she just wrapped her hands round her mother and held her tight. She needed to hear everything her mother had just said.

At the beginning of her sixth month in the hospital, Desire was discharged. She could now come to the oncology unit on out-patient basis. She was also supposed to continue physical therapy for twice a week. She was now back on her feet. She was doing a lot better and relating to everyone better. As for her cognition and learning abilities she had lost, she was gradually picking up.

Well, she got discharged from the hospital to see that there was a new family member which was me. She had been seeing me around, but now, there was a formal introduction. I was the family member assigned to her by my amazing support group and she could always call me up to talk to me. I was also supposed to visit them at home at least once in two weeks, but thanks to my relationship with Mandy, I was around more often and always available to help in whatever way I could.

I had totally enjoyed my time with the Greens and as much as I was volunteering and it was work, I learnt so many values from them and just became a better person on a personal level.

Desire was going to continue receiving treatment for the next two years and some months. I was happy to see her return to school. Her classmates had been educated on how they needed to be supportive as she was just recuperating. Well, she had new classmates since she had lost part of an academic year. Her new classmates were warm and welcoming to her. As for her, she was glad to be out of the hospital. I don't think there are people that exactly like hospitals. I just think everyone that goes there just has to. I am not the only one on my boat; that gives me joy. I still do not like hospitals.

CHAPTER THREE

*E*ven money and being able to afford the best possible healthcare can save one from some things. One of those thing is being at the final stage of breast cancer. In stage zero of breast cancer, it is just a warning sign and although there are abnormal cells in the area, they have not spread. In the first stage (stage 1), the tumor is minimal, but the cancer has not started spreading. In the second stage (stage 2), the cancer have begun to spread, but the tumor present is minimal. Stage three is quite an advanced one and although the tumor may be large or small, it would have spread to several lymph nodes and caused skin ulcers and inflammation. Stage four is the final stage, which is even more advanced and the cancer has spread to other parts of the body.

If a person's breast cancer has gotten to the fourth stage, it is advanced and cannot be cured or treated. The individual just continues to get treatment to ensure they stay alive. It is the terminal stage of the cancer and the person affected generally has between 3 to 5 years for their survival.

All the time I was working with the Greens, I was also seeing other patients and their relatives. I mean, I have been seeing many patients simultaneously and it was about four months after my initial signing to volunteer with the support group (the six weeks of training inclusive) that Desire got discharged. I was trying to live my life too; hanging out with Fiona and some of her other friends she had introduced me to. However, it didn't just seem to be my thing anymore as much as it used to be. I was seeing life in a different way. I was seeing life through the eyes of my patients. Fiona was volunteering too to fill in for someone, but I cannot say she was going through the same journey I was going through. She was also getting to see patients and we were relating on that level, but I seemed to have a deeper connection and concern for the patients I was seeing. I knew this from our conversations. She was seeing life differently too, but she thought I was becoming too attached and rather too serious about each case. Perhaps, a part of me that I didn't even know was in existence was coming out.

The day I met Fatima. I was devastated. She was seventy-one at the time and had just retired from running her business. And no, she did not retire on her own accord, if she had her way, she would work up to the age of 80 or maybe 90. Her real estate business; she could run it over the phone now that she had become as successful in the field as anyone can think of being. She had struck several deals with hotels and multinationals. She had done so much in her career and not just in her career, but also with her family. You know, it is quite easy to get jealous of another person's progress, but if only you know the journey that took them to the height they have reached, you would think twice and try to get rid of your envy. Her husband had died after only 10 years of their marriage. She was only 34 years old at the time. She had three kids; Halima, Jubril and Yusuf. She could not afford to see her kids suffer, so after many months of mourning her husband, she picked up the pieces of her life and real estate degree, as well as the remaining pieces of her dream which she had pushed aside to raise a family. She started her real estate business and did all she could to spread her tentacles as far and wide as she could. No matter what, her kids were never going to go hungry. She wanted them to live without feeling the absence of their father who had always done everything to make them comfortable, before he passed away.

She continued to work hard and give her kids her good life. Fatima never easily took a day off work. Her desires had heightened. She wanted her business to never go down; she wanted to build an empire that her children's children would thank her for. She thought that since she had come this far in establishing herself in real estate, she might as well make it legacy for her generation. So, she worked harder. She had sleepless nights strategizing and hardly took off time to rest.

As for her kids, they did not disappoint her one bit. They got those amazing degrees and made her very happy. However, none of them was exactly ready to go into that line of business. In the hopes that one day they would be interested, Fatima did not relent in putting in efforts for one moment. She kept giving her all. She had extended her business to many countries and so she had to travel a lot. However, she did not bother so much about her health. Her thoughts were that she was very physically active; being as up and doing as she was unlike many of her age who were living a sedentary lifestyle. She was exercising and using her multivitamins too. She was not supposed to need any special check-up or extra medical care. She was doing everything advised by her doctor to ensure that her vitals were normal. Left to Fatima, she was all good.

Little did she know that she already had metastatic breast cancer. This is the final stage of the disease. By the time she noticed discharge from her nipple, swelling of her breast, and a dimple in her breast area, the cancer had already spread, as it was in the final stage already. Fatima was in Dubai when she went to the hospital to report her concerns. She didn't agree with her diagnosis after several tests and scans, so she decided to wait till she was back at home in the states to confirm her diagnosis. When her doctor confirmed that she was at the stage IV of breast cancer, Fatima decided her mind that they were wrong. It could not be happening to her. It had to be something else. She was living in a state of denial. So she created a different reality for herself. If what the doctors had said was not true, something else had to be true. She called her an old friend to meet up, so they could go for a vacation. Her friend, who she had not contacted in about five years was surprised and just thought something was off. She was in another city, but decided to have lunch with Fatima the following weekend. She was going to travel down to see her friend that was usually too busy with work to catch up with anyone or anything else. She knew that there had to be something more to Fatima calling her. As they sat over drinks that weekend, Fatima revealed the real reason why she had called to her.

"The doctors say I'm dying. I'm at the final stage of breast cancer." She had said.

Marilyn, her friend, pressed to know some more and it was then that she found out that she had not even told her kids about the cancer.

"I told Marilyn that I do not have cancer. I told her I was too sure that it was some little disease and the doctors were only trying to blow it out of proportion." She giggled as she told me.

Marilyn kept it to herself at first, but at the end of the weekend, she realized that she could not stay with and care for her friend as much, so her children really needed to know the situation of things. She advised me to tell my kids even if I did not believe what the doctors had finalized the diagnosis to be.

"Your kids are the closest humans to you. Even if you still do not believe, whatever is going on with you, your kids need to know. It doesn't even matter if it's a small problem that would be gone in a while." She had said. "There was something in me that knew that this problem was here to stay for a long while, so I'd rather create a different reality that did not include me having any bad news to break to my kids."

She continued to be in denial. However, cancer is no nice disease. And with breast cancer in its final stage, it was more like having a ticking time bomb, waiting to explode within your body. Her denial did not take away other symptoms such as the fatigue, pain, difficulty sleeping, shortness of breath, anxiety, digestion difficulties and depression away from her. It did not stop the cancer from spreading into her liver and causing abnormal liver functions. It did not stop her skin from yellowing or getting itchy, it did not take away the abdominal pain either. It did not stop the cancer from spreading to important organs in her body like her lungs or her brain. She could deny it, but it was there.

"Two weeks after Marilyn's visit, she called in and realized I haven't told the kids, so she called in and told them by herself. I was going to fight her for this, but I didn't even have the strength to, in spite of having a nurse who always came to care for me. I really didn't want to become that grandma that gave everyone trouble. The kids were doing well in their careers and building amazing families. I did not want to ruin that for any of them by being a burden. This was in spite of the fact that Jubril and his family lived in my city. I did not raise them just to be a burden to them, you know."

"You can never be a burden to them. Family is the unit that stands by you when things go south. You are their mother and they cherish you." I said to her.

"I know. Now, I know these things. Before, I really felt like I was being a burden to them."

The process of getting to this place where Fatima could talk to me was no easy one. Once she realized her diagnosis had come to stay and was not about to change, she became unexpectedly angry too. I mean, this is usually the case for many cancer patients, but when it hits close to home, trust me, you'll be surprised too. She had given so much to get the best out of life. She had sacrificed so much to achieve all she had achieved. She had taken no holidays and paid attention to being healthy, but because she had not paid attention to her breasts, now she was suffering, she was in pains. This is the hard part about being diagnosed to cancer, there is no one to be angry at, and so cancer patients just get angry at life in general. For weeks, she was angry at everything, and it showed in terms of how she related with people. She was mad at her own body, turning against her, after all she had already been through.

"It could be sometime during the day, when I would get a call about a test or the result of a scan; another negative report. Why me? Why did it have to be me? The worst part of it is the fact that there is no exact cause that can be tied to my cancer. I have never heard of any female in my family that had it, so why did it have to be me? Life had already dealt me quite a huge blow at an early age and I dealt with it with so much courage, so why again? There are so many women all over the world with no serious issues. I have friends and acquaintances who have had it easy all their lives; they came from a rich home, had a great education, great friends, married an amazing man, have beautiful careers and are enjoying their homes in their old age. They have not had to go through the serious life-changing issues I have had to go through."

From what she was saying, I could infer that she felt that life felt like…"Oh, you have the strength to handle that much pain? Now, take some more. It was a crazy kind of reality for her. She left the anger stage and later moved to the stage of bargaining about things she could have done better in the past to make her current outcome better. She talked about how she reflected on her life night after night. If only she had taken her check-ups more seriously and not felt like nothing like this could ever happen to her, perhaps, she would not be in her current state. When she realized that it had come to stay again and no matter how much she tried to bargain, she could not turn back the hands of time, then she sunk into a well of sadness that seemed endless. Jubril and his wife, Mariam took turns at coming to stay with her, yet it didn't change much. By then, she had started treatment. She had decided to go to the hospital just because everyone would be bothered if she didn't. Yet, she kept being lost in her thoughts and caught sighing from time to time and totally forgetting there was anyone around her at all. Her kids were calling more often. Halima and Yusuf were also taking turns at spending weekends at her place, and sometimes, with their families, just to keep things lively.

"It gladdened me especially when mama got a point of acceptance. This does not mean she was fine with the entire idea of having the cancer, but she just woke up one morning and began to show signs that she was ready to fight this thing by herself. She seemed to have made peace with the fact that she was now in a different phase of her life and she needed to do what was necessary to survive through the phase." Halima had said.

"She seemed to start looking forward to her treatment sessions" said Yusuf.

"And she finally agreed to stay in a private room in the oncology unit, which was our best bet at monitoring everything going on with her." Said Jubril.

I was beginning to wonder myself why such grown-ups would want to talk to me about their struggles. Well, I had invested time in learning how to listen and counsel patients and caregivers in the oncology unit. However, it was still surreal and felt very much like a blessing.

They had so much confidence in me and so did Fatima. I liked it and I looked forward to going to Fatima's ward every day and talking with the family. Jubril had represented the other kids in employing capable hands to run the real estate business. They all now played different roles in ensuring that the business did not get affected by their mother's unavailability in any way. They did not like how sick she was, but they had quickly adapted to the current situation so things did not get worse. We had talked earlier about how if they showed that they were very affected by what was going on with their mother, she would only feel worse as she was already bothered about not being a burden to them. That was another role of volunteers in helping cancer patients and their relatives. They could not tell their mother some of the things they told me and she could not tell them many of her worries concerning them too. And although that is privileged information which I am not allowed to directly share with either side, it influenced how I advised and the kind of advice I gave to them. All that advice really worked and I was very happy to be part of the process.

The painful part about Fatima's story is how she never got to enjoy life. She was too caught up with the many problems that came with life. Then, she ended up old and sick. That's harsh to say, but it is the truth. Each time I saw her, I felt so sad that she did not gave to taste the sweetness of life in spite of having the means. She was so engrossed with work, growth and her kids. This taught me a very important lesson about life.

Life is quite unpredictable. Everything could be fine one minute and in the next, there could be chaos. She had achieved a lot in terms of her career and raising her kids, but now that she was supposed to be more relaxed (irrespective of if she was building a legacy or not), she was supposed to be enjoying vacations and time with family. At least, that was what the kids said she had planned. However, this was not the case for her, she was now nursing a condition that she would have to nurse till her last breathe. She was getting the very best possible treatment in St. Greg's (as a renowned facility), but that did not mean she felt no pain. She was in a lot of pain and her survival depended on all the treatment she was getting. I just wished that at seventy-one, she had been resting. This particular story taught me to remember to enjoy my days while I can. While working so hard to achieve anything in life, do not fail to deny yourself of pleasure at every point in time. Even if it is the smallest of pleasures you can afford at the time, remember that you truly deserve it. I was rooting for Fatima. I kept rooting for her.

"I walked in on Lucas cheating that same night."

"Oh no, you didn't."

"Yes, I did and no matter how much I try to erase the memory, it still lingers because that was the day I knew for sure what I was dealing with."

"I am so sorry Anna."

"Thanks." She giggled. "I don't want to pretend like it's alright, but every day, I wake up and decided that I am going to fight this thing and I just want to be happy no matter how things go in the end. Dwelling in unforgiveness would definitely make me unhappy because I would be holding myself captive too when I don't forgive."

I was quiet because I knew she had more to let out.

"You see…with Lucas, it felt like I was with my soulmate. We were loved up to the point that I completed his statements and we knew the passwords to each other's social media account. I did not just catch my ex-boyfriend having sex with another woman, he was making passionate love to her, with romantic candle lights, scents and roses all over the place. That said a lot. First, it was definitely not their first time as they would have probably been more careful. They were just so confident that no one would catch them, because they had done it so often and never been caught. Second, it was a well-thought out process. It was well-planned in his house. This means it was no mistake. He knew I was going to be home all night because I had said I wanted to be alone when the result of my final test was emailed to me. He knew I was going to be home and probably grieving. I only changed my plans last minute only to see that he had been cheating all along. That had to be the most painful day of my life. I was not winning on any side that day. I just wanted to go up to his apartment and get lost in his hands, but he only showed me that I had never been enough for him."

"You are enough. That's his loss."

"Yeah. You know, I used to be that friend that would say those kinds of things to my friends, but it took a bit of time for me to accept that I am truly enough and everything was all his fault. He was supposed to be the best boyfriend on the planet. He always appealed to all my love languages and treated me like a queen every single time. Our breakup just happened when I was at my lowest point, so I kept feeling like perhaps, I should forgive him, but he didn't even give me any reason to actually do so. When he came to apologize, he could not come up with one single reason for me to forgive him. Perhaps because there was absolutely no reason for me to do so. It felt like he wanted to go back right into her arms. For me, I could not afford to be battling with my health and still wondering on the side if the person I am with really wants to be with me. At that point, I knew I really needed to let go. It was hard and like I said, I am still taking it one day at a time, but I think I am a lot stronger than before." She smiled.

She smiled even though she didn't exactly have many reason to do so.

"I admire your strength Anna." I said to her.

She smiled yet again. "I really do. I don't think many people will be strong enough to handle everything you've handled."

"I should be flattered Gabby, but I'm here wondering how many 22-year-olds have to suffer dealing with stage two of breast cancer.

"Anna, I insist that you are a fighter."

Now, she just smiled and kept quiet. She wasn't going to fight me anymore. The nurse had come to check her vitals, so she resolved back to laying on her bed and looking up, just as I had met her when I came in.

By the time the nurse was done, she sat up and said to me, "You know, I keep blaming myself for these things. I have been very thorough in terms of living my life and like my parents would say, my youthful exuberances. I would smoke anything and everything available to be smoked. I drank and drank. I partied as hard as I could. I left no stone unturned in doing all the crazy things in the book. I was really that girl that live frivolously and enjoyed every bit of it. I only calmed down on everything when I met Lucas." She placed her hand on her head.

"I am sorry that I keep bringing him up."

"Oh, it's alright. Remember, I'm here to listen, so keep talking to me."

She smiled. "I think I fell in love with him; completely. I forgot my partying ways. I only wanted to attend the parties he was attending and spend my nights with him. I was no longer in multiple relationships because of him and he promised me the same. He seemed to have fallen in love with me, but maybe I was wrong. Or maybe life is just punishing me for the way I lived."

"No, that's not true."

"Let me speak Gabby. Just hold on and listen to all I have to say for a minute. Gabby, nobody is supposed to have it as easy as it has been for me. I have always been one of those geniuses. I never read as much as the nerds, both in high school and in my few college years. Yet, I have done better than them in exams. I have really wealthy parents who meet all my needs too. I have no need for money, yet I got so many scholarship opportunities. Maybe the kids from school hated me so much and cursed me."

"You are not to be blamed for all these Gabby. There are many "ifs" I know you could think of, but that's no way to live. You have a life to fight for in front of you and thinking this way would slow down your pace."

The bulk of all I had to do here was listen more and talk less. I also had to correct wrong notions. She was at the bargain stage of her grief and she really needed to go through all the stages by herself no matter what I had to say to her. I had to give her time to process all her emotions by herself. I was only supposed to provide help, by being a sort of outlet for her. I could tell her that she should have a smoked less, drank less or checked her breasts for lumps after every period of menstruation, but she could not go back to the past and she now knew these things, so flogging her twice was not going to help one bit.

"Gabriella, when I first realized that I had breast cancer and it was in its third stage, coupled with the fact that my boyfriend technically broke up with me, guess what I did—I threw a party. Do you now see the kind of person I have been?"

"You are a great person, who was trying to process all the grief she was going through."

"I thought throwing that party would somehow help return my life to what it used to be. I thought throwing that party would make me feel better about my health, but after the first party, I realized that the party had only been for a moment, but the cancer had come to stay. So, I decided to throw more parties. I still thought more parties would make me feel better. A part of me wanted my ex-boyfriend to see o social media that I was doing very fine, but I doubt he cared at all. I didn't see him view any of my stories, but I viewed his and saw him having fun with his new girl. Guess what I realized, I had been living for others all along. All those parties were to make me feel like I was a part of something; that I belonged somewhere. I wanted to always feel like one of the cool kids and probably no one saw that, but on a subconscious level, I made it a point of duty to keep being a cool kid. So, I threw parties, attended parties and all that. Once I was diagnosed with cancer and even up till now, it has dawned on me that I never lived for myself. It had always been about what others thought. Gabby, I do not know if I would be able to finish college. I have not lived at all."

I gave her a warm embrace. I was not in her shoes and there was nothing I could say that would take back what had happened or the mistakes she felt she had made, but a warm embrace says to a person, "I am here for you."

"Moving on, live for you. Come what may, live for you." I said to her. She nodded and then smiled. I was glad that what I had said at least meant something to her.

"I would live for me and nobody else." She said in between her sobs. "Thank you Gabby."

Her parents were very happy that at least their daughter had someone to talk to. They were the typical rich parents who hardly had time to monitor their only child, not because they didn't care, but because they had businesses to run and their child was now an adult. They wanted her to live her best life without any restrictions from them. She was doing well in school, so they provided her just everything she needed to live her best life. Anna was fine with that too. There were times when she missed them, but she had her friends and then, she had her boyfriend.

Anna could continue school if she wanted, but she had decided that she would hold on for at least one school year, as she could not cope with the emotional stress that came with people wanting to know what happened to the version of her that liked to party. She just needed sanity and that meant being on her own for the time being. She had seen how her supposed friends reacted to her condition. They treated it like she had some plague after hearing it from another friend. They hardly came to visit and when they called, it was about telling her how they shopped or they partied, knowing fully well that she could not do any of these in the moment. They showed no empathy for how she was doing. So, in spite of knowing she would be cured in about 18 months or at worst, two years, Anna decided that she would stay off school for at least one year. At least, in that year, she could get her mind together. Returning to school almost immediately would just remind her of her woes, as she had realized that her supposed friends were not even her friends. None had come to sit to have a heart-to-heart with her. She could now see that they were all a bit broken and had been thinking that partying would fix them up. They had been wrong. If one does not have friends to talk to in trying times, then you do not have friends at all. They were yet to realize this, but her own woes had made her realize the fact first. She was more grateful than ever for the gift of me and she thanked me with each passing moment.

She could not seem to stop talking about her breakup with Lucas. That was the worst of it. Losing your backbone in your trying times is the worst thing that could happen to anyone. I listened to everything she had to share with rapt attention. Her parents were now more available, but they did not even have as much access as I had to her rants. They did not seem to know so much about what had been going on in their child's life all along and they were now sorry. Speaking to Anna, she was not angry at them either as she had always been that child that liked to keep the details of her life private. She took absolutely no offense.

"You know, Lucas should not have done what he did because he was with me when everything started. Like one of those other nights, we were on the couch. It was another Netflix and chill night and he began to hold me tight. He held me so close to himself; it was harder than he usually did or maybe I was the one who felt more pain that I normally would. At first, I screamed on the top of my voice, and he wondered what had went wrong with me. I wondered if it was pregnancy, but the tests came out negative. I had learnt that pregnancy could make the breasts very heavy and hurtful from one of my girls that got pregnant. The test had been negative, so I had no reason to worry. I was supposedly fine, but the pain was still there. It won't go away." She paused and drank some water. We were in their home, as she was going through stages of chemotherapy, but only staying in the hospital when it was necessary to do so.

"Should I ring the help up to get you some juice?"

"No, I'm just fine."

"I insist. I have so much to pour to you today." She giggled. "It's the least I can do for your troubles."

"Okay then." I cackled.

After Lydia brought some juice, she continued.

"Lucas was the one who insisted that I had to go to the hospital to check out whatever was wrong with me. And so, the next morning, he drove me to the hospital as early as possible. Well, I thought that was so sweet...the way he cared for me and had my back. He had felt a warm bump and that was what I felt when I touched it too. On getting to the hospital, I was examined and the female doctor said it could be an infection of my milk ducts, but those kind of infections are usually found in breastfeeding mothers and the baby usually sucked it out with milk. On getting home…" she said smiling. "I called up Lucas and he made jokes about making a baby if that was what it would take to get the infection out of my system. I found that really funny, but maybe cute."

"Honestly, that's cute, considering the fact that you loved him."

"Uhum." She said, staring into space.

"Then, what happened next?" I said, stroking the back of her hand to call her attention back to our discussion.

"Well, I told him the doctor had given me pain medications and antibiotics for treatment, so maybe we could make those babies later. We laughed hard that night. Gabby, it was really cute. The drugs did not do much, there were no changes in how I felt, so the next day, he picked me up and drove me again to the hospital. The doctor kept saying I was a 22-year-old and we shouldn't be looking at a cancer. I did not have any hereditary link for it too, as I had started asking my parents questions at this point, but when they asked what was happening, I said I was just doing some research and it was nothing for them to worry about. Again, I had always been that child that figured her shit out on her own, so it wasn't surprising that they let me be." At this point, she began to sob.

I did not try to hold her. I recognized that this was part of her healing process, so I let her let it all out. "Let it all out." I said.

She continued once she was ready. "They did an ultrasound and said the radiologist would have to read it and then, I had two very painful biopsies to ensure that a wrong diagnosis isn't made." She paused and held her lips because she was about to burst out in tears again. It was as though she was trying to hold all her pain together, as though the pain was trying to split up, but she wanted it to come out in one single unit; as her tears.

"Gabby, the moment I got that mail that evening. I just wanted to run into his arms and cry. A call from the hospital came in, for follow up counselling I guess, but I didn't want to hear any of it. I didn't want to think of the whole process of chemo and this might sound vain, but the hair loss!"

At this point, she had shaved all her hair and my guess was that a lot of it had fallen off during chemotherapy. I had seen pictures of her with her. She was a blonde that you could really call "Becky with the good hair". I did not understand her pain, but I could see there was so much pain in her eyes. She was going to continue her treatment process of course, but the cancer had changed so many things about her and definitely her life view.

I was 18 years old and she was 22. I just kept thinking that this could have happened to anyone. By the time I am 22, there would be so much I would want to do with my life and having a cancer??? It was definitely not on my list, but Anna had done nothing out of the ordinary; nothing a girl of her age would not do. It made me wonder how much of control we have over our life. Perhaps, the saying that we only have influence and not control is very true.

CHAPTER FOUR

used to hear that people came from Africa to America for treatment, but I never took it seriously. I used to see many people also donate an even some donate a portion of their properties to people going through health challenges in Africa. Also, I have read severally that the money pumped into many parts of Africa is not evenly distributed because of the corruption there.

All these things never really dawned on me until I met Betty. People often talk about men dying before their wives, but what about the wives? What happens to them after their men are gone? I talked about Fatima whose husband died at a young age earlier. Here's Betty whose husband died when she was 60 years old. She had a drinking problem at an early age and once her husband passed away, she sunk back into that state. She continued drinking and drinking. Her life did not look like it would get any better as she was really lonely. She hardly wanted to talk to anyone and the only reason she did not take her own life was because of her daughter. Her family insisted that her daughter stayed in a boarding school pending the time she got better, but she only got worse. She kept drinking. She had treated liver cirrhosis at an early age and she was warned about the efficiency of her liver as she grew, but that was the life she knew.

"Life got hard after my husband died. I felt like taking my own life severally. John was my all. He was my knight in shining armor. Life was great with him. He didn't want me to work hard or do anything too strenuous. He just wanted me to look beautiful for him." She smiled as she spoke. "I used to drink a lot before I met my husband. He made me stop drinking; drinking was once my addiction after my parents died, but my husband became my addiction and I stopped drinking. For many years, I hardly thought of drinking, but once he was gone, the thoughts came back again. All I wanted to was drink. I knew I was putting myself in danger, but I was torn between staying alive for my daughter or dying because my husband was gone. I did not want to see anyone or talk to anyone for many days. I am just happy my daughter was put away and safe. People kept saying I had to stay alive for her and that was my only source of strength." She said to me that afternoon.

When they diagnosed Betty of liver cancer, she was not exactly surprised. She had been doing everything that predisposed her to the condition, considering the fact that she already had a liver cirrhosis in the past. Her daughter was in high school at the time, but she had a few months left to be done. She had a tumor on her liver and needed to be operated. Without telling her daughter, she went in for the surgery. However, the surgery was not successful in their country. She had used all her savings and the money her husband left behind for the surgery. She just wanted to stay her alive without her daughter, Meriah, having to deal with the fact that her mother was sick just after her father had died.

The surgery was unsuccessful yet her health kept declining. She kept getting worse and was paranoid about having another surgery. She talked to a family friend that had removed a lump from her breast earlier and she advised that she tried getting a surgery in the United States of America.

"The United States?" I asked. "How am I supposed to afford that? I definitely thought she was joking, but she went on about how no amount of money equated the worth of my health. I felt even guiltier about the fact that I had put myself in that state and Meriah would be the one to suffer being an orphan if she lost me. However, there was no money. Yet, my paranoia got worse by the day. I had several dreams about dying and going to join my husband where he was. However, it was just the paranoia. I would wake up afraid and angry; angry at the lot life had casted on me. Maybe it was my fault that my liver was failing me, but my husband did not deserve to die in that accident. He was such a good man and good people should not die like that. I wished I could turn back the hands of time and I had been the one in that accident. At least, I would not have cause to make Meriah suffer having a parent with cancer. At least, I'd be dead and not even have to imagine what having a tumor on my liver felt like. My husband would also be alive, being a good father to our daughter. I could trust him to be that for her. The long and short of it however, is that I had no money to treat my condition. That meant only one thing, I had to resort to what people in my country used to do. I had to start going to crusades. Perhaps God would heal me. I would go to church."

"You would go to the church and pray to God for healing, but also ensure you get a surgery to get well again, right?"

"No. In Africa, many of us believe that God can heal us and we have to do nothing to secure that healing. We simply have to believe."

"I understand you." I said to Betty. "I attend mass too and I know that faith without works is dead. God has given certain people (healthcare professionals) the knowledge and the skill to care for people that are ill and all you have to do is ensure you submit yourself to be cared for. You talk to God to help use those people to care for you, especially if you do not have enough faith to get a total healing. If you do not follow these principles, the rest will really be left to you; it's not on God anymore."

"Hmm…Gabby, it took quite a while for me to realize these things. It took a while for me to realize that I actually had to go and get treated. For many months, I attended vigil after vigil; crusade after crusade. I was really believing God for my healing. I did everything I was asked to do. I bought several items from many prophets thinking it help my healing.

They sold several items, but little did I know that it was all for their own gains. They were trying to enrich themselves all along." She paused like she had something more important to say.

"Gabby, if you look at my back, you would see several marks." I checked and the marks were so many.

"What did you do to deserve this?"

"This was from a prophet who claimed he was going to beat the cancer out of my system. He beat me for about four hours that particular day."

"What?!! And you thought that would somehow heal you?"

"Yes, I thought so. That was how I endured all that beating. As he beat me, I kept thinking of my daughter and how she would not have to worry about a parent that has cancer. I kept thinking about how I would set my daughter free. So, the more he beat me, the more I submitted myself to be beaten."

She told me how she was slammed on the floor severally by another prophet that promised that she would be healed after he had slammed her on the floor. It made me wonder why anyone would subject themselves to that kind of trouble, but I guess it was the desperation to get healed. Betty told me how many people would come with different health conditions (including HIV/AIDS) even without using antiretroviral drugs, in the hopes that they would be fine after being slammed on the floor by some prophet or given a bottle of water to drink by a self-acclaimed man of God. It was painful to me to hear how fellow humans were going through the worst because of their illness and their ignorance. I wished there was something I could do to educate more people in Africa, hearing that there were lots of people who believed that these things were true. It was an absurd way of thinking, but I could relate it to the poverty rate in that part of the world. If people had more money and were exposed to better options for healthcare in that part of the world, this would not be the case for many. They would be in hospitals, looking to get healed rather than being in churches and hoping some miracle would happen. Of course, I believe in miracles, but

Betty had ended up discovering that many of these self-acclaimed men of God were actually out there to put take the little many of these people had. She had eavesdropped on a conversation some of them were having by chance and it was about calling for more offerings so they could make more money to take home from the "crusades" the organized. It was heartbreaking for her. It was also at that point that she decided that she needed to look for an actual solution to her problem—the medical way. After all, she had been attending the crusades for six months and her symptoms were only getting worse. There had to be another way around getting healed.

"I think I put my faith in those pastors and the crusades more than God himself. He was the healer, not them. I could as well pray in my home and get healed, but it was better if believers come together. However, the gatherings I attended were fake, because the intentions behind them were never about us getting healed. It was about how much they could make off sick people. Anyway, I had no strength left in me to pray to God after all my ordeals with them. I just wanted to be left alone, but since my health was only deteriorating, it dawned on me that the tumor was still there and I still needed to seek adequate help medically. However, I had no money to do so. I used to bake in the past, but how much would I make from baking bread that would be enough to bring me to the states here, for surgery? How much? I was in pains and definitely could not bake as good as I used to, so things were in fact a lot worse."

She had to play her last card. Betty had to do it and that was why she did it. She started selling everything she could sell. From everything in the house that cost a lot of money to the personal effects of her late husband. It pained her to do so, but he would want her to be alive to care for their daughter. He was so fond of jewelries, so she sold the jewelries he had left behind. It felt bad to do so, but she did it because she had to stay alive. He wouldn't want her to die right after he did. So, she was able to come to the United States, to get her tumor removed. St.

Greg's hospital had come highly recommended, so she opted to use the hospital. That was where I met Betty.

Everything had seemed to happen in a rush for Betty. It was all in the same year; her husband dying, being diagnosed with cancer and going utterly broke. It was not something she had found courage to talk to until now. Even now, she only revealed her story in bits. The truth is that she needed to talk to a shrink, but all she could afford was to be cared for in the hospital. She could afford her surgery to take out the tumor and then a small part of her liver and nothing else. That was all she could really afford. So, the sessions where I listened to her were really important to her, because she was at that point where she just wanted to talk about everything that had been bothering her.

"Many things ran through my mind when I started experiencing weight loss, I lost my appetite, I started vomiting and felt nauseated often. I also had a swollen abdomen and white, chalky stools. I went to the hospital and I was told I had high bilirubin levels. I knew for sure that it was related to my liver and I was given drugs to treat my symptoms while I ran tests. In the end, I got diagnosed with a tumor on my liver; liver cancer. This was one month after I reported to the hospital. Well, that was one of the worst days of my life by I took heart knowing that I was only being rewarded for living the way I had lived. After taking the surgery and it failed in Africa, I felt like I was going to lose my mind. Now I can talk about it like it is nothing, but it was a lot back then. I felt like I was going to go crazy if no solution was going to come."

Betty's daughter came with her to the United States. She was done with high school at the time her mom was coming and so, she came with her. She stayed with her mom in the recovery room most of the time. My support group had provided her shelter to stay in the United States as they had made no provision for that while they were travelling.

"I was really scared that I would lose my mom when she insisted that she could only get the right treatment for her condition in the states. We have never travelled out of our country to any other country in Africa, so coming to the states just seemed like a lot. I mean, it was the first time I would hear her say she was sick and then we had to travel to get her treated right. I also noticed that she had to sell so many things in the house to ensure she could pay for the treatment. My dad's death made me realize that being alive was the first and most important thing. My mom's sickness ended up making me realize that fact even more."

Betty and Meriah felt better about the outcome of the surgery. They were just grateful to have each other and you could now see it in how they looked at each other. They looked at each other with so much love; they were all they had and they were never going to take that for granted.

"I am just happy that I was able to get over that phase of my life successfully. I wonder what would be my fate now if I still decided to stay somewhere in Africa and believe that I would be fine miraculously. I now understand that God has provided the knowledge for many problems to be solved and I hate that I put myself and subjected myself to a lot of trouble, merely out of ignorance. When I decided to come to America, it was not as thought I was 100% sure that everything would be fine, but I prayed to God and decided to give it a shot again. Where I come from, putting yourself under the knife meant a lot. There would usually be an entire prayer team holding a vigil for you to ensure you come out safely. However, now, I have realized that it is our system that is faulty. Life is harder on our end and we have to pray to God to keep us safe from many things that are supposed to be very much in our own hands. I was scared that I had subjected my liver to a lot and too much of my liver may be lost again with another surgery, but now, I am thankful to see that everything is just in good condition. I would never take my life for granted again and this experience would leave me never wanting to drink again."

The last statement Betty made was a lie. She was definitely still going to crave drinks severally. Hence, my support group let her join our meetings for alcoholics while in her private ward. She could join the meeting using her phone. She seemed to be committed to her new resolve to stop taking drinks. She was really grateful for her life and did not want to take chances at making Meriah lose her. She confessed that whenever she looked in Meriah's eyes, she was ashamed of living the way she had lived. She apologized to her daughter severally for her behavior, but the young girl who I was just a year older than was quite mature. She chose to understand her mother's plight without giving her much worries. She was just happy to see that her mother was doing a lot better and had responded to treatment perfectly.

This particular story again reminded me that the fact that things are fine somewhere in my bubble on one end of the world did not mean that things were fine all over the world. People were indeed going through a lot and contributing my quota by being a listening here was indeed the least I could do.

I have never met a cancer patient as optimistic as Lynn. Her story was supposed to be every girl's dream story and cancer just had to come ruin for her.

"I was just happy that my surgeon here at St. Greg's reassured me that I would be just fine following the surgery and a few sessions of chemo to ensure all the cells are entirely dead." She said excitedly to me.

I could not even imagine being in her state. What was there to be excited about considering the fact that she had to put her beautiful life on hold because of cancer? I could not just imagine being the one in her shoes, but on the overall, I chose to draw strength from the woman she had chosen to be. The kind of optimism she shows was second to none.

"I admire your strength and optimism." I had to tell her. "Keep it going Lynn. You are doing a great job at fighting this."

"Don't make it sound like that Gabby. Although I have always been the positive girl all along, it has taken a lot to get to this place in my life since the time I was diagnosed. Right now, I am just grateful that my surgery went well. Trust me, I have many things I do not like and I wonder how I would live with. The scar from the surgery has always been of concern to me even before the surgery. I am just 28 years old and I have always said I wouldn't like to have a C-section once I am ready to have babies because I just hate scars. I didn't want any scar, but here I am. And trust me, I don't like the fact that I now only have one kidney. I wish things were different, but since this is the place I find myself, I have decided to embrace it and just make the best of it by not wasting any other day of my life sad or depressed."

I used to think she was not so bothered even after she had told me her cancer story, but now I could see things through her eyes. What could be worse than going on a romantic trip with your fiancé in Greece and taking in beautiful sights, only to excuse yourself to pee at dinner and find blood in your urine?

"It was such a heartbreaking day for me. Trust me. However, I thought it was nothing serious, considering the fact that I lived healthy. I hardly ever smoked, I took alcohol occasionally and in minimal amounts, I also loved to exercise and I had a very active lifestyle on the overall too. It was definitely not my period, so I ruled that out. It had to be something else. I told my fiancé and he told me not to worry too much, but to be sure to check in with the doctors once our romantic weekend in Greece was over. I am glad I enjoyed that weekend to the fullest, as it was the last vacation I could have till my treatment was over. I was only 28 Gabby. I was trying to live my best life with the love of my life and everything seemed to be stable until the sickness raised its ugly head. Once I got back in London, I went to see the doctors and while I made my complain, they were sure to remind me that I had nothing to worry about. After all, I was really young. In their opinion, it was probably an infection, but they ran tests and found nothing. However, in the meantime, antibiotics were prescribed and administered. I used my antibiotics religiously and carried on with my life as they had advised. They told me not blow things out of proportion with my actions and just keep living, as I had nothing to worry about." She paused to drink a glass of water.

"I went to work as usual and continued with every other aspect of my life. However, the pains in my lower back continued too. It was specifically on one side of my lower back. I also felt tired. The symptoms had only subsided for two days after I started using the antibiotics before coming right back. It continued up to the point that I could not go to the hospital anymore. I lost my appetite and weight loss followed. The blood in my urine did not stop as well and soon enough, I began to feel feverish too. It was a horrible place to be for me. On a certain day at work, in the middle of a presentation, I felt so much pain in my lower back and I was so uncomfortable that it became noticeable. Luckily, my boss who is quite lenient discovered that something was off with me and decided to come up with some excuse about why we needed to bring the presentation to a quick close. She took it upon herself to ensure I got home safely that day. It was embarrassing and a few people had begun to notice, but she really saved the day for me."

"Thank God for such bosses. I noticed how she came to see you yesterday and even brought you flowers. I was indeed surprised that she was your boss."

"People don't know how far the little things they do mean so much to people like me in times like this. I mean, I experienced an unexpected change in my life, so I know how much I appreciate every form of help that comes around; even the unexpected ones. I appreciate those even more. My boss was the first to tell me I needed to take time off work for the time being. I know you're young Gabby, but I'm sure you have at least heard a little about corporate work spaces and how people just want you eat you up on those streets. People just want to kick you out of a job, but my boss has just stood out from the rest, especially in these times."

"What happened next with the doctors?"

"Gabby, there is something about you and your entire body language that makes me want to spill out everything I have ever wanted to say. I don't know what it is, but I like you and I like talking to you."

"I'm flattered."

"No, you have an amazing presence. I'm just saying the truth."

I was lost for words. Only a smile could rightly express how I was feeling in that moment.

"I went back to the hospital and of course, I complained about my symptoms that won't just stop. I told them in details everything that had happened to me in the past few days, including my ordeal at work and how I could not even go to work anymore. The doctors reassured me that we only needed to take things one step at a time and I was young so it was not likely to be too serious. I believed it was nothing serious, just as they had said. They scheduled me for an immediate ultrasound and also booked me for an appointment with the urologist. It was at this point I began to get a bit concerned about what might be wrong with me. However, like I said, I am this person with a positive attitude. I have never been one to joke with affirmations and all that. I was also receiving a lot of support from my fiancé who was always on phone with me most of the time. Luckily, he works as a freelancer, so he could call me on his schedule when I was home and couldn't go to work. Anxiety was killing me right before my urology appointment, but he was there on the phone and came around when he could too."

"You got flowers from a fine young man that came around two days ago. That must have been him."

"That's right. He came to see me right before catching a flight for a work trip."

"How cute!"

"Don't get started honey." She smiled. She was apparently very in love with him. I could tell it from her smile and only hoped that someone would make me smile that way someday.

"The urologist was so nice by the time I got there. His suspicion was that it was a kidney stone, so once again, he reassured me to take it easy with my worries. He was going to examine me alongside the initial ultrasound scan I had done. That he did. On doing this, he noticed that I had a swelling on my kidney and let me know. My heart was torn into pieces. I kept asking many questions, but the question that topped it all was what it meant for me to have a swelling on my left kidney, which happened to be the kidney on the side of my back that ached badly. Initially, when he suspected a kidney stone, all he was going to do was confirm and do a surgery to remove it immediately. I thought we were going to do the surgery soon enough and then I would be fine once again. Everything in my life was on hold, my life had come to a halt for the time being. I thought things were about to get better and I was about to pick up, so you can imagine how disappointed I was when he said there was going to be no surgery for the time being. He said we would have to hold off on it and then run another CT scan the following day to confirm what he assumed it could. However, he asked me to refrain from being panicky in any way. I asked if it could be cancer, but he told me to keep my age in mind while I had all those thoughts. He told me I was quite young and the likelihood of cancer was very slim, so I should really refrain from worrying. At first, I had a couple of sleepless nights, but later on, I began to stay positive. I decided to stay positive. I stayed close to those that loved me and they kept reminding me that they were with me and I had nothing to fear."

"I have seen how much your family and loved ones have supported you in my short time of staying with you. I have seen them give you quality support. You have built quality relationships Lynn. It speaks a lot about the kind of person you are."

"Well, I cannot say I am perfect, but I try my best to stay warm and kind. I love the people around me; I always have, and I stop at nothing to show them this."

"It shows Lynn. You also have a very strong and positive spirit. It is admirable. I came here to hear you out, but you already seem calm. You are warm and affectionate in spite of everything going on with you."

"Gabby, I have seen people become assholes to others because of a situation they have found themselves by chance. For me, I just decided that no matter how hard it was going to be, I was not going to let my circumstance make me treat people badly or stop being the warm person I have always been. I have imagined having a few days to live on earth and even if that ever turns out to be the case for me, I don't plan to live my last days being nasty."

At this point, Lynn stood up and walked to the window. She paused for a long while, just staring at the sky and just taking in the view before her. I let her have her moment. I knew she needed sometime before she talked some more. It was nothing new for me at this point. I had seen patients do this many a time.

"Gabby, when it was confirmed to be cancer, it was as if my entire world came crumbling at my feet. For sure, I did not like the sound of it and for the next few days, of course, I was angry and confused. I did not deserve that out of life. I was that girl that was always on her best behavior. No! I deserved better from life. I was so angry and more shocked because I was quite young. I mean, I just clocked 28 at the time. However, in spite of how I felt, I needed them to just do the surgery immediately because my symptoms did not seem to care about my feelings one bit. I just needed the surgery to be done even after I was told that it actually meant losing one kidney. They had told me that I could survive okay with one kidney, so I was just going to find my way around that." she paused again.

"C'est la vie Gabby…that's life! I had to move on and find a way to forge ahead without being too scared of what would happen next. I was told that the tumor was malignant and not benign too. Prior to that, I was thinking it could be a benign tumor and I wouldn't have to worry much. It was just my way of staying hopeful. The malignancy was why the surgery to take out my kidney had to be done. Additionally, the lymph nodes close to my heart had been affected too. Gabby, I did not want to die, I agreed that everything be taken out as soon as possible. However, you know how things are at St. Greg's, the doctors are usually in high demand. I would have to wait for another one week to have my surgery done as the person who was supposed to lead the team was quite a sought-after doctor and was not available to do the surgery immediately. At first, I was heartbroken and then, my anger heightened. I wondered why life was just unfair to me. I was having a rollercoaster of emotions; one minute I would be angry and in the next, I would be optimistic. The people around me had to be very optimistic that I would change at some point and realize once again that they were on my side. I don't think I knew how to change at the point. The positive me was so weak and I had given into my every emotion. I was the nasty person I said I didn't want to be for those 7 days. As much as I tried to control that attitude, I also realized I didn't just have the know-how. I had never experienced anything so unfortunate in my entire life. It was my first time and I was not doing a great job at it."

The first time Lynn got hold of her emotions after that time was when she met with her surgeon. This was two days before the surgery.

"There was something about the way he spoke to me that was just very calming. He reassured me that I would be fine and everything about me would be back to how it used to be in a matter of time. However, he was not unrealistic. He told me that it would not be perfect, but I would return to being very much like me. He also said the lymph nodes would be taken out carefully too and I just needed to be at rest. I asked if he could speed things up for me a little, but he reminded me that things had to be done on schedule to avoid mistakes when it came to human life. There was something about the way he looked at me that made me know that he was the perfect guy for the job and I was indeed in good hands."

"Did you go back to being positive?"

"Yes, I went back to being positive. I had read about the stages of grief and I had tried to control myself into each stage as much as possible to no avail. However, after I had met with my surgeon, I realized that I was in the acceptance stage of my grief and I was just ready to go through with everything necessary to keep me alive. Trust me, I still thought about the scar a lot and how it may even affect my self-esteem as the young woman I am, one who likes to live her best life, but c'est la vie! I was more open with my family, friends and fiancé on how I needed them to be more close to me. I focused on other positive facts like the fact that the cancerous cells had not spread to other important organs in my body and could still be contained. Then, I set my mind on my open surgery and the twelve weeks of recovery I would need following the surgery."

What surprised Lynn the most was how her happy girl attitude went to shit at that point, no matter how hard she tried. It was really nice to meet Lynn. She was definitely the kind of person to make a bitter story look like it was a sweet one. She was a hundred percent the positive friend that everyone should have in their circle, but in spite of how positive she was, cancer had shook her a lot. I was just happy to see that throughout her twelve weeks of recovery, she was getting all the love and care she deserved. She was now also more open to sharing her story than she was earlier on when I started talking to her. It was glad to see that her mind was healing too. She was a hard and smart ass worker at her job and had found favor with her boss, so above all, she had a job still waiting for her after the entire ordeal.

CHAPTER FIVE

"You don't ever do anything right. What did I get myself into?" said Lily as she paced from one end of the room to the other. "I don't deserve a man that does not even know how to get me gifts or make me happy? Look around, look at our friends. Do I need to remind you how your friends gift their wives with cars regularly?" Her breathing became more rapid at this point.

"Shame on you Patrick!" she said, as she moved away from the kitchen table.

"Henry may hear this. Don't wake him up with such harsh words."

"You are concerned about our son? Really? I am surprised, because if you truly are, you would find a better means to provide for this family. When I decided to get married to you, was my lifestyle not obvious enough for you to see?"

"But you know I'm trying. I am sure you can see I am trying hard to make my source of income better."

"Patrick, you are not trying enough. There should be more you can do. Men out there work hard to keep their families financially buoyant. Patrick, we have just one child yet you struggle so much. I have had to use my money to ensure things stay balanced and I have even taken on an extra job."

"Lily, we both know it was my recent investment that went in a way I did not plan. If things went as planned, you know that in spite of the fact that I have lost my job, I would still be able to cater to all our needs. Just give me some time."

"Patrick, I have given you so much time and you really had to wait till now when I have run out of patience. Look, when there is a will, there is a way. Don't tell me there is no way to make things work financially. Don't tell me you need more time."

"Lily, what has come over you? You used to be very supportive. You know that I am sincerely trying my best with finding a new job or picking up something else I can do. You used to have my back. We got married because we were best of friends. What is going on with you now?"

"Patrick, you took me for granted."

"How?"

"I feel taken for granted by the fact that you still feel comfortable that you don't have a job. And it is all because you know that I am buoyant enough to take care of our needs."

"You got it all wrong. Lily, I have my struggles. Lily, of course you know I don't like being like this."

"No, I don't!" she replied sharply. "I don't know that."

"Wait a minute, do you still love me?"

"Patrick, I should be the one asking that. Do you love me at all Patrick? Did you ever do?"

Patrick had taken the most he could take. He felt like she was trying to provoke him all along and now, he was ready to give in. He was ready to give in and do just what she wanted.

"Guess what? It's hard to love a woman that keeps acting like this."

"Oh! I am hard to love now?"

"I didn't say that." He said, shaking his head and realizing what had just came out of his mouth.

"That was certainly not what I meant and you know it. I just need you to act better. I mean, Lily, we've been together for six years."

"Oh! You've been counting often and I can see it. I can clearly see that you are tired of me and this entire marriage."

"Oh! Lily, what has come over you?" He said softly, as he moved closer and tried to rest his hand on her shoulder.

"Patrick, what are you doing? What are you trying to do? Why are you even trying to touch me?" On the last question, the tone of her voice changed and she sounded really harsh.

At first, Patrick felt like she was just being stubborn, but now he could see that she was not planning to end the quarrel anytime soon. In fact, it looked like the quarrel had just started. There was a long moment of silence and that silence was as sharp as a knife. He stared at her and she stared just back. They looked each other in the eyes sternly, but Lily looked at Patrick more like a vulture looking at its prey. She had made up her mind to hurt him that day, in return for the hurt she felt even if he had not hurt her on purpose.

"Lily…" He said calmly. "Can you remember the first year of our marriage? Can you remember how happy we were? Can you remember how supportive you were of me? What changed Lily? What changed? Why have you become so harsh towards me in my time of need?"

"Patrick, please stop acting like a saint. You know I have always been the one out-doing myself. It was because of my family's influence that we even got a chance to move to the states! Wake up Patrick! I have always been the one doing so much. I don't even know if you loved me when you said you wanted to marry me or you decided to do it just because of the benefits."

"Don't say that Lily."

"Well, all that does not matter anymore Patrick. Here's what matters: I am sorry, but I don't think I am in love with you anymore. I don't think I can do this anymore either."

"What do you mean by that Lily? You can't do what?"

"You'll have to figure that our Patrick."

On saying this, she went into the visitor's room and locked herself up. It was 11:15p.m. She was going to sleep in there that night and leave the next day. As for her things, she would send a pick-up service to pick them up. Lily just wanted to go away and never look back anymore.

Patrick was not expecting what the next day handed him. He had gone to sleep the master's bedroom upstairs after he realized that his wife had locked him out and there was no plan that could get them to talk again that night. He went to bed thinking that they would talk things out the next morning. He woke up the next day to see the door of the visitor's bedroom flung open with his wife nowhere in sight. He called her name, as he went to the kitchen and then outside the house to see if she had gone for a run or something. He found no signs, so he came back inside once again, to the visitor's room. It was then that it dawned on him! He just knew for sure that Lily was gone and she was not coming back.

In spite of this knowledge, his heart won't just stop racing. So, he decided to call her. He called severally, but she won't just pick up the phone. His calls went straight to voice mail.

Lily had left with nothing, but her purse, her phone and her handbag. He could not help, but wonder: *"Was that how much she wanted to run from me? Was that how much she detested me? Was that how much she detested the fact that she had Henry for me? Didn't she think of what leaving would do to our son?"*

She had never seemed like the type of person that would throw in the towel and run just like that. At least he had never seen her that way, or maybe it was just the love he had for her. Maybe.

"Where is mummy?" said Henry, as he ran down the stairs to see his father staring into the visitor's room. "She didn't come to tell me to get up early and dress up for school today."

It was at this point that Patrick really wanted to cry. How was he supposed to carry one with the responsibilities of two people?

"Oh! Is that so?" He asked, trying to sound as composed as he could. The tears were about to come, but he knew he had to be strong for his son. His son was too young to handle the fact that his mom did not want to be with them again. It definitely sends across the worst kind of message to a 5-year-old if the child even understood what it meant for her to be gone for life.

"Oh, your mom had to leave for a business trip early this morning. She would be back soon."

"Aww…she didn't kiss me goodbye." He said, looking sad. "She didn't make my oatmeal too."

"Daddy would do all that." said Patrick, as he lifted Henry into his arms. "Momma loves you, okay? She just had to rush."

Henry nodded. He was actually used to his mom not being around. The only thing that had bothered him was really the fact that she had not said goodbye, and she hadn't also made him some oatmeal before leaving, but daddy would make it, so he was now smiling.

"I would also let you take some ice cream later this evening, since mommy is gone for now, okay?"

"What if mom finds out?" Henry whispered into his father's ear.

"Let daddy handle that and give me a high five." He said to his son who totally loved this plan of theirs.

For the next few days, the fact that he had to be emotionally there for his son the way two people had been there was what actually weighed him down a lot. The physical aspect was something he could definitely handle. He bathed Henry, picked out his clothes, made his meal and packed him lunch with no issues. Then, he went to the meagre jobs he did at the local store, including running shifts and the counter and sometimes cleaning. First off, he had to make enough for the survival of himself and his son even if they could not afford any luxuries for the time being.

However, all his efforts including the extra job he took on did not stop his son for continually asking about his mother and saying how much he missed and could not wait for her to come back. It was hurtful that his child would think that way about a parent that did not think that way about him anymore. However, all he had to do was cheer Henry up and lie to his face over and over. He had to lie that she was coming back and that she loved him, but it was all for the good of the child.

Henry did not fail to remind his father about his mother at every given point. Every night when his father tried to put him to sleep and even tried to read stories to him, he would emphasize how much he missed his mother putting him to sleep, but there was really little Patrick could do about that he just kept giving his best in the way he knew how to.

School events were not left out. Patrick tried to represent his mother at events which his mom was obviously supposed to attend, but his efforts were not just sufficient. To crown it all, he had to cut down on many luxuries his son once enjoyed and it hurt him a lot that he could not afford those luxuries.

It was a slap on his face that nothing he ever did was just enough. He just finished he was dreaming and someone would wake him up from the nasty dream that was making him feel so miserable, but nothing changed! Nothing!

So much time passed by that Patrick hardly had anything to tell the child anymore.

"Dad, where is mummy and when would she be back?" Henry asked another time when his dad came to pick him up after the close of school." He had begun to look like a liar to his child, as he had been promising that his mom would be back for months, all to no avail.

"She came to my school that last time we had a sporting event. She promised to be around this year too."

"Oh! Is that so?" said Patrick as he brought Henry into the house.

"Well, mummy has been so busy this year. She said I should fill in for her."

"…but dad, mom would always call and speak to me on phone no matter what happens. She likes me so much and does not like to see me unhappy." Patrick looked at the five year old handsome child and wondered what he and Lily had done to deserve such an amazing offspring in spite of their own shortcoming. However, he was sorry; he was really sorry that he was going to be breaking the heart of his son. He wondered how he was going to actually tell his son that his mother was gone and he was not sure she would be coming back any more. Even without telling him, it had been showing that something was missing with Henry. It was not only his child that was asking for the whereabouts of his mother. Those in the neighborhood, teachers from school and so many others were doing the same. Each time Patrick was asked in the past, he would say she was on a business trip and would be back soon. However, many months had now passed and it did not make sense for her to be on some business trip for that long. It was obvious that something was very wrong. He had been saying Lily was on a business trip in the hopes that very soon, she would show up and say she lost her mind the other day and had missed her husband and her son. He was hoping she would come around to say she was sorry for all she had done and had realized that they were all that really mattered to her and not the little things she complained about. He longed for her to really say that he had just been going through a phase and had been a great husband before them. He hoped that by the time all these happened, he would then have a chance to settle things with her without external parties knowing what had actually happened in their marriage. So, he had kept saying she was on a trip, just to make sure their relationship stayed intact when she was back, but she did not even come back and it did not look like she was going to come back. Patrick had quite a number of sleepless nights wondering if he could finally tell his son the truth. He did not want to be the father that lied and gave his child a false childhood. As much as he wanted to be a responsible adult, he could not really take responsibility for the fact that his wife had left. It was no fault of his. They had their disagreements and all that, but it had been her choice to go without saying good bye. Hence, he came to the conclusion that he would give their child an idea of it. He would have sought counselling and professional help if he had enough money, but he did not even have enough to spare. He didn't have the luxury of it in the moment. So, he wondered what his best bet was. He could lie that his Lily was sick and in some hospital in another country, but that was yet another lie and he was definitely going to end up hurting his son if he lied yet again. He might also give his child a horrible childhood and he had grown with a father that had done things he was not sure he could forgive. He certainly could not let his son go through the same, as it came with a lot of burden and was certainly not a good place to be. No…his son did not deserve a childhood filled with lies. However, sometimes when the truth is told, it comes with lots and lots of pain and he was not sure Henry could deal with all that pain.

Yet, the performance of the child in school work and other activities just kept dropping. Things were spiraling downhill for the boy and Patrick thought that it was much related to the absence of his mother. Patrick himself was dying on the inside, wondering how he was going to break the news to his son. He hardly had any friends to talk to about what had happened considering the fact that he was waiting for his wife to come back and get reunited with him. He did not want to spoil that mix. He had also had a disastrous couple of months (especially with the loss of his job) and he did not have the bandwidth or mental capacity to break yet another bad news about his life to anyone at all. One more round of bad news over drinks with friends and he was too sure he was going to lose it and that was the last thing he wanted…to lose it. But here's one thing he did not want even more: to mess up his son who had been having a great childhood all along.

One afternoon, when Henry asked again, he just kept quiet.

"Dad! I miss mom. When is she really coming back? Tell me the truth daddy."The young boy had said, shaking his dad's body vigorously. It was obvious that the boy just wanted a honest reply from his father on when he was going to see his mother.

Patrick drove to an affordable ice cream shop and got his son some ice cream while he asked him to sit and take some. He was finally going to tell his son the truth after six months of back and forth.

"Dad, is mom sick? My best friend's mother is really sick and his daddy takes him to get ice cream a lot so he can feel better about missing her. Dad, hope that is not what you are doing." At that point, Patrick really wished that was what he was doing; he wished he was going to even tell his child his mother had a sickness that she was treating and that she was going to be home very soon, just because she loved him so much and could not just wait to be back with her family, but he doubted she even remembered they existed. His calls just kept going to voice mail.

"Your mom is gone." He told the boy. He did not know if the five year old understood the implication of what he said at all or the boy just read a totally different meaning to what he had said. Immediately he said those words, Henry dropped his ice cream spoon and tears began to stream from his eyes. In school, they had been thought at their early age that sometimes mom and dad might have to be separated, but it did not mean they did not love him.

Patrick wanted to tell him he loved him and his mother loved him so much, but he did not want to tell a lie by chance to the child because he did not know if Lily still had one ounce of care for the child. Henry cried all the way home too. He wouldn't just stop crying. Patrick asked him if there was anything else he wanted, but he really wanted nothing else. He just wanted to go home, crawl up in his bed and sleep.

The worst part for Patrick was when his son had asked if he would at least get to see his mom sometimes and he could not even guarantee the young boy about that. He just kept quiet and then he shook his head as he could not even find the right words to say to his son and the time he eventually felt like he would say something, he felt like the answer was too harsh that he would be breaking the heart of the young boy beyond measure. So, he summoned enough courage to just stay quiet and yes, that took quite a huge dose of courage, as something in him just wanted to scream out loud and tell the child the entire truth. Henry, as little as he was, locked his room and cried throughout the night. He cried till he fell asleep and once he woke up in the middle of the night, he began to cry yet again. He would not let Patrick in, so Patrick fell asleep at the door of his room, hoping that at least he would see him once he decided to get out. The evidence of his cries was visible in his eyes; he had such swollen eyes the next morning from crying and not being able to sleep. Patrick called in sick at his son's school and at his workplace the next day. Father and son had been heartbroken, but his son's own was a more recent one and Patrick knew that he would need some help in feeling better for sure. He was just going to stay at home and cook all the favorite meals of his son for the day. However, no matter how hard he tried, Henry would not just speak to him. Now, he wished he had enough money to book a proper baby sitter while he went to work, but he did not just have enough, so he had to take on the role of babysitting his son as an extra job.

The next few weeks, as Patrick described were not great. The summary of the most it was the fact that Patrick was now lacking in terms of all his school work. He was not just doing badly at his curricular activities, but he did not also want to perform extracurricular activities. He did not want to talk to his friends either. He was just withdrawn from everything altogether.

Patrick tried his best to get through to him and know what was going on with his son, all to no avail. The harder he tried, the harder his son seemed to withdraw. The teachers in school had noticed and Patrick was now going in for every possible meeting with all the emphasis being on how his child was doing horribly at school work and other activities. Patrick felt so helpless, yet there was very little he could do. Hence, he just broke down when he met up with friends of him and Lily. He told them everything that happened, which had been keeping to himself for the past six months. He told them all his fears and his worries and he became far more relieved than he was before. He wondered what had kept him from not telling them all along; probably shame. However, he was not even in the place to be ashamed of anything he had done at all. It was Lily that left, she was the culprit and even though it really takes two to tangle, his actual worries, were not his fault. They were Lily's fault, for the fact that she had chosen to leave him. Perhaps, it was not even supposed to be a thing of shame for her, but it was not supposed to be a thing of shame for him either.

All of a sudden, Henry began to fall sick. At this point, Patrick missed Lily so much, but the situation being what it was, he had to lock up the way he felt and just keep it all to himself. On some days, his son developed the flu and it was severe. On some days, he just had cough symptoms. On others, he felt like vomiting or sometimes, his stomach just hurt so bad. It was quite a trying time for Patrick as they were always in and out of the hospital. He hadn't ever seen it coming that his child would be that sick. All possible tests and scans were ran to rule out different disease. It was thought that the boy was a sickler, but on continual tests, it was discovered that there was nothing in his blood that indicated that. At first, they addressed the sickness by symptoms. They treated each symptom per time. Drugs were administered for each sickness he came up with and at some point, conclusions were being drawn that pershaps, it was just a developmental stage for him. All the time the boy was sick, he did not say so but Patrick could sense how he really wanted to have his mother by his side. Sometimes, it is usually downplayed, but the role of the mother in a child's life is very essential. As jealous as Patrick felt, he remembered his own childhood and how it was the presence of his mother that made it possible for him to go through all the trying times when he felt like his father did not want them. Each time he thought of his late mother, the thoughts were of warmth, comfort and assurance that someone always had your back. He was sorry that Henry did not have that kind of relationship in his life, especially at that particular time when he was now sick. He had considered getting married to another woman, as Patrick's mother had sent him divorce papers a few months back to his surprise. He had been really thinking that she was going to come back to apologize up till the time when she had sent those. The papers also came with a letter that let him know that she had moved on. The content of the letter provoked Patrick to the point that he decided he didn't want to have anything to do with Lily anymore. If she wanted to go indeed and she had started a new life like she had stated, it was fine. He only hoped that she would at least grant phone calls, so their son could speak to her. He wrote her back and had it delivered to the city she had moved to. However, she never called and his calls still went to voice mail. His smart guess was that she still felt guilty about leaving their son behind, at least if she still had any decency left in her, she would feel that way about what she had done.

The long and short of everything was that Patrick had decided not to get married again for the time being because he was yet to heal from all that had happened to him. He was not even financially buoyant enough to do so, even if his son needed it. After they got married and moved the United States, he had to take some courses, so he could be integrated into the work environment. This made him have a whole lot of student debt to settle off. He was still paying all those loans back when he had lost his job, so the last thing he wanted to do was take on more credit that he would have to pay back or incur extra responsibilities by thinking of another marriage. Luckily for him (unlike most men), his divorce had not cost him anything. Lily must of have thought of him as very worthless as it was obvious that all she cared about was leaving him. She did not care for one day about gaining anything from the divorce and that kind of hurt his ego, but the truth was that he had nothing to give either. He was also too stressed with all his own life troubles to want to see Lily for damages or the terms under which their divorce had happened. If he had the resources, he'd probably find out the details of the new person she was seeing and use it against her by bringing up the subject of infidelity, but that happened to be the last thing on his mind. He really just wanted to move on and take care of Henry.

Additionally, if he was going to get married, he had made up his mind that he was going to get married to someone he loved and not just because it felt okay to do so, for a random person's companionship or because his son needed a mother. He could not deceive anyone. He didn't even have the bandwidth or emotional strength to deceive anyone into a marriage, considering everything he had been through himself.

Now, the long and short of everything was his son—all that really mattered was sick and they were still yet to place what had happened to the young boy. As they kept treating the symptom, they kept dismissing anything serious could be young with the young boy. Then all of a sudden, one day in school, after doing a few extracurricular activities (which he was not even doing well at), the young boy collapsed all of a sudden. He passed out and everyone got on their feet. They rushed him to the hospital and had his father on his way to the hospital already. Once they had him back, they did an MRI on his brain immediately. It was at this point that they made a very shocking discovery that was going to change Henry's life. It was discovered that the young boy had a tumor in his cerebellum (a part of the brain). So, it was essentially a brain tumor. Patrick was devastated. He wondered if there was anywhere lower than where he had reached in his life. He couldn't take it in anymore. He couldn't hide how he felt about everything that had happened.

He made for the hospital hallway and screamed, "L-I-L-Y!!!" People thought he was losing it and they tried to calm him down. He almost became hysterical and started calling Lily over and over. It kept going to her voice mail, but he would not stop calling her.

"She cannot just leave me with the responsibility of two people" He cried out in the hallway intermittently. He had also called a few friends out of his confusion. He was not even sure of who he was speaking to each time someone picked up the phone, but he just kept talking about his son and what they had diagnosed him with. In a short while, his friends were around and the doctors told Patrick that an emergency surgery needed to be done on his son. Patrick had never known agony the way he did on that particular.

"It should have happened to me and not my innocent boy." He kept saying. He felt Henry had already been through a lot too; seeing his parents separated and worse still, waking up one morning and never seeing or hearing from his mother anymore. Now, he had a tumor in his brain and it was a cancerous one too. First off, they had to remove the tumor and then, after the surgery, they had to check and be sure that nothing was wrong with any other part of his body. They had to be sure that the cells had not spread to any other part of his brain, head or body. The operation was going to be 16 hours long at least and while he thought about how to cover costs, he was told that Henry's health insurance would cover for the surgery, but not the treatment they envisaged following the surgery.

Patrick tried to hold back his tears, but he had been through so much that he cried like never before. It was all he could do in the moment. He had two friends wait with him while the surgery was on. All the while, he kept calling Lily to no avail. Now, he wished he had taken the clause in their divorce agreement about taking care of their child a bit more seriously. However, since he used the services of no lawyer, he had taken things lightly since he was too tired of everything that had been going with him and all that had happened with his ex-wife too. Again, he had just wanted to let go and never look back, but here was a twist in events. Here was a twist he never imagined was coming to him. It was a twist to their story that he did not think he could have done anything special to block off. He had gone online to see if he had been guilty of anything that put his child at risk for having that tumor. There were lots of people saying exposing a child to too much technology could do that to the child, but he was not even guilty of doing that. They did not even have as much luxury, so why would that happen to his own son.

Cancer? Why him? After everything he had been through. Friends tried to console him as Henry was being operated but there was little or nothing all that consolation could do. They did not know how he really felt, so they definitely had no idea how to console him. They were just trying and it was not exactly helping. As the parent of the affected child, he was the one going through the grief stages. Although the stages were faster for him since reality had to dawn on him earlier (thanks to the immediate surgery that had to be done), but he was going through those stages of grief anyway and he could tell that none of it was nice.

The surgery ended up being successful and when everything got checked out, not much was left to be done, just some radiation and the entire chemotherapy process. Patrick was a bit relieved by the outcome of the surgery and the chances for recovery, yet, Patrick could not afford it. Hat in hands, he ended up having to beg friends for all the help they could render. It was indeed one of the lowest points of his life, but he just had to do it.

His child was going to be in the hospital for another six weeks following the surgery and there were going to be lots of expenses to ensure he received the best possible care. So, he took all that help from his friends. All the while, Lily was still ignoring those calls and he could not help but wonder if it was the same woman he had known or if he had just married a stranger.

Now, he was glad that it was all over because he looked back and imagined how he had coped being married to someone that had such a horrible attitude. How do you abandon people you once claimed to love and called family just like that? It was indeed depressing for him to think of all that, but the best he could do was to keep his eyes on the future and of course, keep his eyes on his son. He could not afford to let anything happen to that boy and he swore on his life that if he had to beg to ensure the boy did fine in life, he would do so without thinking twice.

He was blessed to have friends around him that supported him in those trying times as soon as he spoke up because the worst thing that could happen to anyone was to have serious problems in life, speak up but still find no one who was willing to help. It was the worst thing that could happen to anyone going through trying times. As I kept meeting patients, it kept dawning on me that bad times do come in life, but to survive them, you just need good people around you. You need friends you can count on, so you can keep smiling even in the dark when no one else is watching, as you have a solid system of support behind you.

CHAPTER SIX

e asked them to euthanize him. I have heard of people talk about this, but this was the first time I would know someone who got euthanized first hand. I had spoken to him on several occasions. He was one of the patients assigned to me and I thought he seemed a little depressed. I had even talked to Diane about him and although, he was not on her list when she was seeing some patients at St. Greg's hospital, she had some amazing tips for me. He was a tall, black man; like with the figure of a basketballer and an amazing family. I had never understood the concept of euthanasia till I saw people go through real pain. People may be of the opinion that asking to get killed was chickening out of life because you have to balls to bear all that pain. However, it is not even that way. If you have seen people go through extreme pain or you have a sick relative, you would understand better.

I'm talking about the kind of pain that is usually a fight between life and death. The kind of pain that makes a man go crazy and that pain was what Michael felt. So here's what I think of him: He's a hero, because it takes a lot of balls to decide that you will choose death over life. Many people go through pain not deciding what they want and that is fine. They go with the flow without a mind of their own and that is very okay because pain could also make it hard for one to decide. From my talks with cancer patients, for sure, I knew that on some days, it felt like you were doing well and combating the illness. On some days, it really felt like you were battling the disease even with your mind and all will be well. Whereas, on some other days, it definitely always felt like they should throw in the towel and just give up, because of their pain and the kind of life they find themselves subjected to, all because of their cancer. There's this back and forth in their mind over and over, but for Michael, he could make a choice. He knew he would go through the physical pain he was going through, as well as the mental pain that most of his male reproductive organs had been removed. I guess it was too much for him to bear and he had really considered the whole point of living if he was going to live with so much pain. When I heard about his death, I prayed that his family will be consoled because that good man no longer existed.

His kids described him as the very best father anyone could have. He was strong, yet very supportive and kind to everyone around him. He had thought them how to display their strength through kindness. He achieved this by working so hard, yet giving his all into taking care of all those around him that needed his help. He provided financial assistance to as many as needed help, sometimes, to his own detriment. He seemed like an angel in human form to so many people, appearing and helping them when they were in need. He gave his all into taking care of those around him that were not as privileged financially. It made them conclude that perhaps that is exactly why he had been born at all—to help people, because he did that so well and felt content even if things were not going well with him. Even when his sickness had started, he constantly talked about how he wanted to help a lot of people. He spoke about all these when he did not even have the financial capability to do so. However, as always, he was just hopeful that the financial capacity would come someday. And while others thought of what they would like to do for themselves when they had the financial capability, he thought of what he could do to help others. I thought it was rather beautiful for anyone to think that way, so did his kids who described their father as rather selfless.

Michael had a strong personality and sense of self. He was not one to do things because others were doing them. He clearly had a mind of his own and lived by his own rules throughout his entire existence. So, it was his own rule that his life should be ended. It was on his own terms, and that decision only showed an extension of his personality. I felt like he would be finally resting, after all the pain he had been through. That was my consolation, as well as that of his family when he died.

"I have seen people die, but this is the first time I knew that someone I loved was going to die because they had asked for it to end their pain. It is a different kind of heartbreak when you are with someone you love and you know that they would die for sure. I could not look him in the eye. We were already mourning him before he was gone because we knew he was going to be gone soon and that hurt me so much. It hurt my mother so much. It hurt my siblings. It hurt every single member of my life to come to the realization that very soon he would not exist anymore. However, it was his choice to make. He was very much alert, but of course, in pain when he had decided that he just had to go and also begged us to respect this decision of his that was going to leave us heartbroken." Said his last child, Tamara.

"Michael's pain had started with pain in his back, but he had always had back pain from years of sitting behind his computer, so he thought it was the long-standing back pain he had always had. Hence, he resolved to do his own self-remedy, like he had always done in the past. He used several pain relief tablets, morning and night. However, his pain would subside only to resurface after a very short while. He complained of the pain sometimes, but we all regarded it as the pain he used to have. It was very easy to dismiss what was going on with him like it did not matter much. A lot of people had back pain episodes, so this was nothing new. We did what family would do; stand by you, get you some medicine if you insisted that that is what you want and later on, advise you to go the hospital. But dad did not think he needed to visit the hospital. He thought the pain would go on its own. It was surprising to see him still going through the same process in six months' time. However, this time, the back pain had become worse and was now limiting his function. There was a limit to how he could walk around, lift things and just go about life. He had always had issues with lifting heavy objects, but it was now worse. In addition to this, now he had begun to complain about pain in this chest area. However, everyone had a little pain in various body parts most time, so he started using more pain relief drugs in the hopes that it would all be gone." Said his wife.

There's a thing about optimism working against over favor. In Michael's case, he was very optimistic about his work and every other aspect of his life. However, when it came to one's health, pain is always an indication that something else was wrong with one's body and it needed to be visited with the right kinds of treatment. You don't have to hide the pain or merely take drugs. It is very important to treat the source of the pain, because if you don't, then you are only trying to block out the pain which is trying to pass across a message that there is something that is not right going on within the body. No matter how optimistic you are, you have to treat the pain because you might be optimistic concerning the fact that the pain would go, but there's a deeper issue that needed to be addressed. The pain might actually go, but do not go on thinking that optimism had worked in your favor as it can as well work against your favor. The thing about cancer is that no one expects it (at least not anyone from the larger percentage of people). For that fact, people walk around merely treating its symptoms.

The chest pain Michael had made it increasingly difficult for him to function. He could hardly climb stairs without holding his back or his chest, but you know the thing about being a male in this world of ours; personally, as a lady, I expect every male to be strong by default. What happened with Michael is that he tried to be that strong man he had always been. He had been thought that as a man, he had to be strong for himself and everyone around him. Hence, even with his sickness, he tried to cover up and act like things were not as bad as they were when in fact, every part of his body was hurting.

"If only we knew he was in that much pain, we would have acted earlier. We would have been there for him, but we thought he was even making out the pain to be more than it was. The last thing we were expecting that he had was cancer." Said Chrissy, his wife.

For his pain, his family decided that they would have a physiotherapist come checkup what was wrong with his back and since there were bony spurs around the area, the pain was said to be from that. However, there was actually more than one cause of the pain. He had prostate cancer and it had begun to metastasize to the back and chest area, but only cause of the pain was addressed (the bony spurs) as it was a common cause of back pain to many. Once it dawned on the physiotherapist that he only got worse with each treatment session, it was obvious that more had to be done. It was at this point that several tests had been run and after a lot of back and forths, it was discovered that he had prostate cancer and when we had realized this, it had already gotten to its final stage. It threw everyone into confusion; that all the signs we had dismissed actually meant a lot more.

"We are so sorry. We are sorry that we trivialized his pain. We are sorry that we made him feel he had to be stronger. Sometimes, I wonder if that was why he felt like the best thing to do was to just end his life. Because he was not getting all the support he needed from us. Maybe that was why he decided that it was best to die than to stay alive and had to go through all our ideals of how strong a man should be. No one should be forced to be strong, especially when they are sick. This is definitely the mentality I am passing on to my sons. We are sorry that we failed him; that we could not be strong for him after he had been so strong for us for many years. He had been strong for everyone even when it was to his own detriment.

"The most painful thing that hit me after he was gone was how hard he had worked to have things as they currently were just before he left. He wanted us to do so well, to be independent of each other and very financially buoyant; we had that and when we did, he decided to leave. Or let me re-phrase that. He was taken away or he was just tired of this fallen world. I am his wife and I have seen him at his best and at his worst. What I can say for sure is that he was indeed one of the best people that happened to the earth. He gave his all and had a vision of seeing his family prosper. Even when he was incapacitated financially, he talked about all the plans he had in place for every member of the family. He had hopes for each child and he had those hopes written out. I just had to get aligned with those plans, get on board and monitor the kids till they reached that level. Every single time, it always felt like I was the strong one. It always felt like I was the one doing everything necessary to see the kids prosper, but the gospel truth was that they had an amazing father who was a visionary and had already seen everything he wanted them to be." Said his wife.

She had been shocked at his death and now that she was finally speaking up after a long time, I was ready to listen and knew enough not to interrupt. She always had that look that connoted that she blamed herself for not doing enough and expecting him to act string while he was at his weakest.

"I wish I did not demand that level of strength from me. And I see that he tried. He really tried hard. He did everything I asked, he showed the level of strength I expected. He did not want to disappoint his woman, so he did everything he could. And sometimes, I even made him feel like he had not done enough. I regret all that. I wish I could turn back the hands of time and act better. I wish I could be more loving. Perhaps, he would still be living."

"It is not your fault" I interrupted.

"I would deceive you if I say I currently believe that. However, what I can say is that I am working towards having that level of believe for sure. And I hope I would feel that way eventually. I hope I would feel like he did not die because of my own negligence. I hope I would feel like I really did all I could in the early stages."

"Mom, no one expected it to be cancer. You did nothing wrong. He did nothing wrong too. The timing of its discovery played a huge role. That's the fact. Maybe there was something more that we should have done, but we did not know." Said her son.

She only nodded in response and stared into a distance.

"He was kind. He worked hard to make every one of us happy and made sure I did not overwork myself while running the home. He was such a hard worker. Whatever skill was new and out there, and sure to bring in money, he gave himself to it. Even if he could not learn that skill or that line of business, he would invest to ensure he had a share in whatever returns on investment were to come. And he did all these to ensure that we did not lack in any way. He stood as a provider indeed and wanted to see no one lack. Meanwhile, he cared about himself only very little. He worried only little about his own needs. When it came to clothes, he got me angry in that aspect because I would buy him clothes and he would give it out to someone who is supposedly in need. Then, I would quarrel with him about the fact that he did not have enough clothes himself. He would promise to get some for himself to replace those he had given out, but my man never did that. He could afford many flashy things, but just remained of the opinion that those things were not for him. He would talk about how many people were suffering and could use that same amount to get their lives into a better place. Well, I would tell him that people would always lack, but we had a limited amount of time to live. I was the philosopher who kept telling him that we were living on borrowed time and we had to enjoy our lives. However, thoughts like that were his own motivation to do good. Thoughts and words like that made him say that he had only a short while to do all this good. If only I had known that these things that he said were real, maybe I would have taken that calling he had to help others a bit more seriously. I would have gotten on board with his plans and made it work even better. I would have supported him in every way I could. The man was such an empath. He came home worried many times about the problems of others and I could not relate." She laughed.

"I knew that there were people that needed help, but I felt like there was a lot of time to help them. But that's why we're humans right. You know, a friend would say that we make plans and God laughs at those plans, because we are mere mortals. My husband was probably one of those mortals that knew how the mind of God worked. He was one of the few special ones among us and it was definitely an honor to be his woman.

"We had just started doing well when he died. I mean, he waited just up till the time where I began to reach great heights in my career, the time I could finally get to afford luxury. It is really painful how he worked hard and lived a life of hardship and now that he was supposed to be reaping all the benefits of working that hard, some sickness took him away. That's the painful part." This was Michael's first child talking. He was a software engineer and had just began to receive massive deals when his father passed on.

"However, I am just glad that he lived to at least see one of my kids. You know, two years ago, I began to do things in a rush. All of a sudden, I met a girl (who is currently my wife) and I got so interested in getting married to everyone's surprise. They had thought I was insane for all the thoughts that were coming to my head and how much I wanted to get married all of a sudden. In fact, my family began to worry about how I was really doing, but you know this inner conviction that just always tells you that it is time to do a certain thing—I had that. And even when everyone thought I was crazy, I still did what I thought was right to do. I am glad I did that because if I didn't, he wouldn't have met my son and I would be in regrets right now. He loved my son so much and everyone could see that. In his last days, when he became very weak, he would ask that Charley came by to see him. He would talk about how the young boy reminded him of himself as a child. He would talk about how he wanted to be there as Charley grew; he told me how much he wanted to see him grow. My consolation is that even though he would not be here to see those things, he at least lived to see my son." The family members were now venting to me even while being rather so quiet with each other. It was as though when their father died, as they were not expecting it, each of them could not find the right words to describe how they felt to each other. However, I, being an outsider with the job of listening to them, they had so much to say to me. The things they said made me think about the death of my father too and I could relate to most of the things they had to say. This is why I knew that my best bet was to sit, listen and make them know that I was really there for them by just being there with them. I could especially relate to the last child, who was looking like he was hurt the most.

"He had plans to be there on my college graduation. You know, we did not agree about the most simple things; like my hairstyle, the fact that I always liked to dress like a hip-hop star, the bling-bling lifestyle he saw that I would apparently like to live and in fact, the list of the things we did not agree about are somewhat endless. However, looking back now, all those disagreements were so useless. I look back and I knew that although he had his imperfections in the way he talked and corrected me, he did all that from a place of love. He did that from a place of wanting to see me succeed and get the very best out of life. All those arguments were pointless. If I knew that he was going to be gone this soon, I would have done everything I could to make him happy always. I would have done what he wanted and avoided arguments as much as I could."

"But you did not know and these arguments are not unusual ones between parents and their young ones. As you know, his sickness and his death was not one anybody expected and again, everything that transpired between you two is nothing out of the normal, so do not stress about it at all. Don't stress one bit."

It was at this point that it once again occurred to me that death was a great divider. Death always really set people apart. It dawned on me how important it is to give people their roses while they are alive. If you love someone, make sure you let them know by your actions. Make sure you say it to them. Don't think you would have forever. Cancer was really teaching me a lot, as a good number of the patients I met did not even have any hereditary link that made that pre-disposed to that kind of cancer. They were not expecting to be sick either. That's the unpredictability of life. We have to deal with that unpredictability by doing what we can when we can. By loving when we can, by making people happy when we can, by being agreeable as much as we can and being a breath of fresh air to all those around us, especially those we love because we never really know how long more we have or they have.

"Thank you for that. You know, I have been blaming myself for a lot of things since he left." Said Damian, the last child. "I keep thinking I should have helped him well all those times he asked for help. I should have helped him better. I should have been kinder, but I felt like he was just trying to make me uncomfortable because of the many things we did not agree on. I felt like I had to keep being tough or he would just keep thinking I did not have a mind of my own. I never really agreed in my heart that he was as weak as he had portrayed and this is why I keep feeling bad."

Again, I reassured Damian that all these things were done out of ignorance and he was just human. He had only done all that based on his own human instincts. He had absolutely no idea about his future.

I asked, "Damian, did you love him?"

At this point, the young man burst into tears.

"I loved him. I really did. I wanted us to not have cause to fight about things that were insignificant in my eyes, but dad is dad. Dad is strict on his ideals of life and there was nothing anyone could do about it." At this point, his eyes lit up brightly like a memory had flushed him. "…not even his wife that he loved very much."

We both laughed.

"Damian, the point is that you loved him. And that is all that really matters. I can see that you really loved him from your expressions too. So, if that is the case, your conscience should be clear and all that. He would want your conscience to be clear and he would want you to live happily. He would not want you to go through life carrying the burden of what you could have done better or worse. Keep that in mind too.

Damian smiled as he stood up. He was in his sophomore year in college and he really looked like the typical cool kid.

Talking to Michael's family got me thinking about my own personal life and family. I could not help but think about my father's death and once again, I wanted to cry. I knew I was going to cry for long and probably cry to sleep. So, I left the oncology unit for the day. I really had to go home and just be alone, but first, I wanted to get on a bus to his graveside, but when I attempted to do it, I realized that I did not have the effrontery to do so. And that was because I was yet to deal with the emotions of losing my father. I was 14 years old at the time he died and arguably a child. I think I was too young to process the way I really felt at the point. Up until seeing Michael's family, losing my father to me felt like having him travel and having that lingering feeling that he was going to be back soon and I had nothing to worry about. However, I was so wrong about that. I had been wrong all along and I had just realized this on that particular day. My siblings and my mom were the very best in that season. Knowing that I was the youngest, they just made sure they did everything within their means to provide everything I could ever think I needed. They gave me the life I had been dreaming of; shopping sprees, a couple of affordable vacations and all the pampering many of my mates dreamt to have. They did all these to make sure that the effect of losing my father was cushioned. However, at the time, no one had really asked the how I felt. And I could understand why they did not ask; they did not ask because they already knew that I wouldn't know the answer to that question. Because I don't know if they really did.

Looking back now, I can explain how I felt at the time. It felt like my father had gone on a long journey and he was going to be back soon. Now, four years after, is when I really realized that he was truly gone, never to come back again, just like Michael. He was no longer with us and I had to accept that painful fact, just like Michael's family had.

On getting home, I said hello to Diana and although she tried to ask several questions on why I was so quiet and all that, I just went into my room and locked myself in. I cried and cried. I cried like my father had just died and my pillow could testify to the volume of my tears. It had finally dawned on me that I needed to accept he was never going to come back and truly move on by letting go of any thought I had left of him. I looked through my pictures with him that night and I smiled as I did. I smiled because just like Michael, he was a good man. So, I became my own volunteer, trying to counsel myself about how I felt about my father's death and why I now had to let go and move on. He would want me to move on. I am sure he would have wanted me to move on far earlier than this, but I was not just old enough to do so. He would understand that. I encouraged myself that night. I looked in the mirror and talked to myself.

Then, I began to write about all my fun memories of him. I began to write about how much of a blessing he was and how my childhood was just perfect with him as my father. I wrote and cried. I wished my mother was round, but since she wasn't, I promised myself to speak to her about him when she was back.

Talking to someone else who could relate to the loss always worked a lot, as I had learnt from my volunteer training. Talking to her would make me assess how much I have healed and how much she had healed too. At the initial stage, some family members did not exactly like to talk about the loss of the loved one to each other, but with time, it happens and it worked differently for some other people. Either way, it had been four years and I thought that was just enough time to talk with mum about him. I actually looked forward to doing that.

CHAPTER SEVEN

"Get out! Just leave me alone. I don't want to see any of you. I want to be alone." Said Sylvia to her group of friends, who had come to see her at home just after her diagnosis.

"We came to be with you and just make you feel better. We just want to be here for you." Said Dammy, who spoke on behalf of her other friends.

"What do you know about being there for me? What would you know about how I feel or how you can make me feel better?

Sylvia was very upset, not really at her friends though. It was more like she was upset about her life and the direction things had taken. She was a bright child and she had managed to get everything she wanted out of life right until that moment. She was in her second year in medical school and her parents couldn't be more proud, to have a daughter like her. She was tall, slim and very pretty. She had registered for some pageants before medical school and while she won one, she had made significant progress in the others. She was the kind of lady that walked in and people got to notice her beautiful stature and her very long legs. She liked to show her legs off, being 6 feet tall. Now, she could not imagine having one of those legs that made her stand out get chopped off. She did not deserve that. This was too unfair and so, she took it out on everyone around her, including her friends.

"You know what? You guys should just leave me and never come back." The door of her room stood between her and four of her close friends, who had come to see her after Sylvia's mom had called them to come cheer their friend up. But Sylvia did not want to see them or anyone at all because she just could not understand what was happening. Why did it have to be her?

"We just want you to know that we are here for you. Every one of us is just a call away if you have anything to discuss, if you need company or if you generally have anything bothering you on your mind."

Now, there was silence. She said nothing for the next two minutes after she had hurled at them to leave prior to that. Her friends had been trying to get into her room for about one hour. They were trying to really be there for her, because they knew that inasmuch as she tried to push them away, she actually needed them and they were there to stand by her.

"We would now be leaving." Said Dammy. "Just call, okay?"

Still, there was silence. She wanted to finally let them in, but her pride wouldn't let her do that after making them wait for about an hour. It would seem like they had won and she believed she was the only one who needed a win this time. She hated that they were going, but she had to let them. So, she sank into the floor and began to think. Where did she get it wrong? Had she done an evil deed that was just too unforgivable by the creator? And her parents! They did not deserve to cry like this. She was their only child and they had given everything to take care of her. And here she was, at 22, doing well in medical school and all of a sudden, she develops an osteogenic sarcoma and she needs to cut off her leg if she wanted to save her own life. She could only imagine how heartbroken her parents were to hear that. Or wait? She knew!!!

Her dad had followed her to the hospital and at that moment when the doctor had said, "You have bone cancer (osteogenic sarcoma) and we would need to cut off your left leg to keep you alive", he began to cry. She had never seen her dad cry like that before. She was not the child that made her parents cry. She was the kind of child that always made them smile. However, this time, the issue was really out of her hands. She had absolutely no control about what was going on with her, as much as she wished she did. She wanted to tell her father that he should not cry and she would be fine, but she did not even know that. She did not know that or what would happen to her next. She thought to herself that she would stay hopeful and just pray, but that was really hard. Immediately she got out of the hospital that afternoon, she realized she was very angry, yet she could not control how she felt. She had many questions and the chief of them was, *"why did it have to be her?" Why not someone from a family with many kids? Why not anybody else at all?"*

Another thing that bothered her was the fact that she was supposed to become a medical doctor and she had never seen any doctor who was an amputee ever! How was she going to run through wards or be very smart in any emergency? Using a prosthetic limb? And will her patients respect the doctor that uses a prosthetic limb? Wouldn't she look like a joke to them? Her worries were valid, yet there were lots and lots of them. She hated her life so much, but there was another thing she hated. And maybe a person too. She should know better, but she hated the doctor that broke the news to her. How dare he talk so loosely? In her opinion, he had talked with no empathy at all. He had spoken without caring how she would feel or how her father who had gone with her would feel. She began to feel like it was personal, but the doctor knew her from nowhere. How she was now thinking was only a representation of everything going on in her mind and she hated herself for that. Anyway, one thing was sure for her. She was not going back to the hospital where she had been diagnosed for anything again. She did not want to set her eyes on that doctor ever again. She did not want to hear his voice too. The thought of him made her angrier than she was about her condition.

And her friends? Did they really know what it felt like to be in her shoes? No, they didn't. And they would never know what it felt like.

And that was not okay. It was not okay because deep inside, she was angry that her friends that had always understood her since childhood will never understand what she was going through. They could only have an idea of it. Additionally, she worried that perhaps, they would say something that would just break her heart altogether. She knew that in times of despair, those that loved you might not know how to console you and this way, their words (if used wrongly) could hurt you the most. She did not want her friends to come in and then say or do anything that would infer that she had brought her condition upon herself, knowingly or unknowingly.

Sylvia used to be this strong girl who kept up with her motivation no matter what was going on with her. She was just the kind of girl that was self-motivated and never needed anyone to motivate her. In fact, her friends used to come to her for motivation and that was one of the reasons why now she found it hard to just rest in their own arms, because frankly, she was the motivator of the group. She ate sparingly, did everything sparingly and had to take time off school. She took the entire semester off as she knew that even after everything was gone, she still needed to get used to the state of things with herself mentally. Going back to school would only draw attention to her and she was not ready to cope with that just yet.

"Am I really going to have to amputate my left limb?" she asked her mother who just got back from her business trip.

"I don't want to lose my limb, mom." She cried, as she rested on her mother's shoulder. Her mother did not know what to say. Or she knew that anything she said at that point would not be comforting enough. She did not want to make unrealistic promises as she did not know if her daughter would eventually have to get that leg away from her body. So, she patted her on the back while she kept whispering to her that she was right there with her and she would be there at every step of the way, so there was no reason for Sylvia to fear. That worked.

The next few months were filled with lots and lots of efforts to get to a better place health-wise. All these efforts, yet there was no results with her leg. Sylvia and her family got referred to everyone and anyone that was said to be able to help her cure the cancer in her bone without having to cut it off. The list of the places they visited was endless, but they spent the most time with a man who had come from India and had promised that he can heal every disease or malfunction of the bone in the book. As she lay there all those months, the growth in her thighs (where the cancer originated from) increased and increased. However, the healer had told them that it was all part of the process and they had absolutely nothing to fear about since they were with him. He kept chanting and had Sylvia lay on the bare, cold floor for about 15 days. She never got a chance to even stand up, sit or walk in that space of time. All she was allowed to do was lay there and listen to him chant over her. Many a time, she fell asleep during the chants too. After three months and her parents had seen that the condition only got worse and she only felt worse, they decided that they had to take her away from the place. There were also several people who had claimed to have natural means to heal up cancer of any kind, they visited those places too, but nothing tangible came out of going there. Sylvia's hope had been raised. She hoped that somehow she would get healed and not have to go to the hospital, but after spending some time with each of the people they visited, she felt helpless yet again and dared to try the next person, till she discovered that none of them actually had a solution for her.

It was quite funny that she was a medical student who had loved the medical field and the abilities that it had to make diseased people have a better quality of life since when she was a kid, but now, here she was, trying to do everything apart from going to the hospital. The cancer had separated how she felt about her own state from how she felt about her profession. She still felt like the medical field and all the learning process that doctors and every other health professional went through was still very valid. However, she did not feel like she was ready to submit her body for a surgery. This made her re-think if her believe in the medical field was as strong as she had thought or it was just a profession she fancied for the aesthetics as well as the nobility it came with. Maybe she was just another hypocrite. Anyway, her condition did not care about her thought process. It kept getting worse.

I have to admit…I felt helpless and it only made me imagine how my parents would have felt more helpless knowing that they could not help their only child get through what she was going through. I had lost a lot of weight and I was generally unhappy. My unhappiness was no news, but at this point, I had sunk into a deeper level of unhappiness that I hated so much. I lost interest in everything around me and it felt like I had lost touch with the things I loved most too. Apparently, I had denied the people I loved so much (except for my parents) my presence too, so I really lost touch with them. I was angry, scared and bitter all at the same time. I did not like who I was at that point, but I was so helpless. I would walk around the house sometimes in the middle of the night, only to hear my mother's sobs somewhere around the corner. It was horrible to know that I had made her cry like that. Like I have always said, I was the perfect child and that did not fall on me by chance. Being the only child of your parents comes with the responsibility of just being the best in everything and bringing them all the joy that multiple kids would have brought to them. Or maybe it didn't. Maybe I was the one who thought it did. And maybe I was wrong, but anyway, it is the belief I held close to my heart. I tried as hard as possible not to feel like I was a failure for having cancer, but I could not help how I felt. On those nights when I heard mom cry, I just wished the ground would open up and swallow me on the spot. The fact that nothing changed made me feel even worse. But did it really matter how much I felt as much as what I was trying to do about what I felt? So, what was I going do with all those negative feelings of worthlessness within me? I mean, I did not do anything to bring this situation to myself, but here I was not even realizing that it was not my fault. I wondered what I could do with all these feelings, but I did not even know I was wondering because I was doing so subconsciously. I was searching my thoughts and trying to put each thought in its place and it was then it dawned on me that I could write. I did not want to talk to my friends who I would have actually talked to about how I was feeling on a normal day, but I could talk to an inanimate object—a book. Many a time, I just wanted to sit in stillness and I did not need to talk to a book, I just needed to stain it with ink. I think I had finally stumbled on the perfect solution and I was ready to take advantage of it. So, I put my reading table in order, brought out a writing pad I had been gifted the previous year and I started to write.

I journaled about the start of my cancer journey and everything I felt at each stage. In the course of writing, I realized all those unresolved feelings I had. The things that I could not express previously, I began to express them in my writing. The thoughts that I did not know were even there were now popping out. Writing for me became like sorting out a really scattered house that is filled with designer items. You know there are designers there that cost a lot of money, but they are so squeezed up that you would not realize which cost more or less until you have properly put everything in their place. It felt like my brain was the house and I was now arranging all those designer clothes, shoes and bags in several categories and colors. It flowed so freely and my head did not seem as messed up again. It is just how you expect to feel after you have arranged a section of this hypothetical house with designer items. You can now walk freely throughout that section of the house. Then, you would be even motivated to pick out another segment of the same house and do the same. I felt better by pouring out my thoughts into that book. I arranged each thought step by step and it was in doing that I realized that I had been stubborn for no reason at all. Why had I chosen not to go to the hospital? Why exactly? Why was I so adamant? As for my parents, they knew I was going through a lot and they did not want to force me to make any decision against my will, so they really let me be. They let me choose, like they knew that I would finally come to this point where I would think about going to the hospital. They had never believed in forcing me to do anything. I know that my mother had phobias for surgeries, so she had said early on, "If she does not want to do it, perhaps it is for the best. Perhaps there is something within her that keeps telling her that it isn't the right thing to do."

So, really, they let me be. But here was I, I had come to the point where I had started wondering why I had made the decision I made at all. Why was I so adamant about not doing that surgery?

"All else has failed and it looks like I would have to run back to the pitch I ran away from. It feels like defeat and that is why I think I am not looking in that direction. It really feels like defeat and I hate losing. Or maybe this hatred for losing is why I hate the idea of the surgery so much. I had vowed to give my life to the medical field, yet it looks like that same field has beat me to it at life."

As I wrote these words, I realized what the real problem was: I had been beaten.

"But was this really about being beaten. Was my own life supposed to be a competition? Did I want to win that much? Maybe, yes, I want to win at life, but definitely not at the expense of my own life. Living was the first and most important thing, then anything else could come after this. Winning comes right after living. The point is, I have to live to win."

Writing actually brought me up from the point I was heading for, even though it was not the point was trying to reach. Writing gave me hope. That little journal was all the therapy I needed, as I had refused actual therapy. My parents tried to convince me on this one all to no avail. But I had found another place to get therapy from and I was enjoying every bit of what I was doing. It made me happy each time I wrote. I felt like I had dropped yet another burden, arranged yet another piece of my life in the best possible way. I felt proud and I filled those pages, it really felt like I was achieving something new. And it made me reach a final decision, I was going to do that surgery at St. Greg's and it just had to be successful, because I had a lot more to do with my life. There were so many dreams to achieve, so many visions that needed my input in life. I could not afford to give up on myself or subject the surgery to chance in my heart. That was the first way to lose and I did not want to lose at the surgery, because winning at it was the only thing that was sure to make me win at life. I always kept it in mind that I had to win at life first. Writing made the surgery, which had seemed like something so foreign, now look very simple. I had written the word surgery so many times that I had now thought to myself that it was definitely something I could do. It was going to be easy; it was no big deal at all. It was going to be successful. I was ready to tell my parents that I was ready.

"I want to go for that operation." I said

My parents just sat at the table for dinner that day. We had been having a few quiet dinners here and there; well, the ones I joined them for. My food was usually brought to me in my room, especially in those times when I wanted to see absolutely no one. I only came out to take it in and on some nights, it took a lot of pleading to have me eat at all. Well, for the nights I joined my parents for dinner, we were all always really quiet and I knew my parents had it that way because they were glad to have me and did not want to say the wrong things. They knew I did not want to talk about what I was going through for a long time and they just abided by my rules. I look back and keep realizing how blessed I am to have parents like them. They were just the perfect parents to have a child like me who would end up with a situation like mine. They knew how to act and they did so perfectly. I did not for once regret having my parents as mine, especially in my time of need. They were the ones I really needed and I was glad that I had them, as the ones who were to watch over me.

"That's amazing!" mom was the first to say. "It was like she had gotten over the way she felt earlier on. It was as if she had made peace with the fact that I might have to do a surgery and it did not need to end horribly. It could go just as perfect as anything in my life.

"I am glad you finally made the decision. Your mom and I are very sorry that you have been through so much. We wish we could do more, but now, we would make it a point of duty to ensure that you get the best care."

"I trust you dad." I said as I gave him a peck on his cheek.

That was how I got scheduled for my surgery at St. Greg's hospital. I did not want to ever set my eyes on that doctor that broke the news to me in that way. I needed to never see him again, hence the resolution to just go with the St. Greg's option and that was the best decision I made with respect to that surgery. The staff were so kind and I was happy that now that I had gotten out of a place of sadness and depression, I was really now in the best hands. I had no regrets coming to St. Greg's; absolutely none. It was the perfect place for me to do my surgery and I was just grateful that my parents had found it.

So, actually, I only met Sylvia because she was back at St. Greg's for having too much fun and getting some injuries on her leg. She just wanted to run all comprehensive tests to certify that she was really fine because she was having way too much fun. She was living like no man's business and her slogan was now, "You only live once" (YOLO). Sylvia who was once upon a time a medical student in her second year, gunning to just finish as the best had experienced a crazy life changing experience. That experience made her this amazing woman who spent the rest of her year after healing from cancer going on several trips and just living her life to the fullest.

"Look, I think the experience I had actually came to make me pause on the way I was living my life. I was only focused on one aspect of my life, but this year has made me see how much there is to be enjoyed, learn from and experience in this world. Our world is a great one and there is so much potential in each and every one of us. I feel happier about life right now with everything I am doing and how things have gone following my surgery. When I had two legs, there was so much I wanted to achieve and I did not even have as much peace as I currently have."

I could see it her. She was indeed a free spirit. When I met her, she saw me talking with another patient. She waited for me to be done and walked up to me to make friends. She told me how conversant she was with what I was doing and how a volunteer had actually helped her pull through those horrible times she actually experienced back then. I felt really proud of myself in that moment. She actually volunteered to tell me her own story out of freewill. She strongly believed that her story will give me a perspective I never imagined I would have. She asked me to sit and just listened to her. She had been checked up and nothing was found to be wrong with her, so she was just very excited and happy to talk to me about her story. She said perhaps, telling her story would help others. This made me ask her if she was already telling her story to some other people she felt it would have direct impact on as well.

She wasted no time in letting me know that she now had an NGO that did just that. She was the owner of the NGO and she was also actively involved in its running as a matter of her passion.

"I am just living my life happily and I am glad that I have parents who support me. I am not saying that I have the absolute perfect life as a cancer patient. I am not saying I don't have days when I cry and wonder how life could possibly be if I had my two legs and I did not have to bother about coming to the hospital from time to time, but I have only made a choice to just work with what I have. I made a choice to pick each day and make it exactly how I want it to be. I made a choice to create all the happiness I want in my life without looking back on everything I had experienced so far. I mean, it is not like I don't look back at all. I just look back without fear. I just look back with the conviction that what happened to me had happened for a reason and I could not afford to let that waste. I had to channel all my pain towards something and now, the way I am living is a source of inspiration to many amputees. I always feel like they hold me in such high esteem that makes me wonder if I am really who they think I am. They look up to me and they feel like they have reason to live beyond all the boundaries and labels that the society has placed on us. I just want to be the best version of myself, for myself and for them. I never knew there would be this version of me until now and I am glad I have discovered this version of me. When your life takes a turn you don't expect, you have to find a reason to stay grateful or you'll be continually depressed about everything and anything. I carry just one real leg with me everywhere I go, so what had happened to me was really nothing I could shut out of my life. I just had to let it be because it was in the body I carried around. This is the same way many amputees feel, but who really cares? This is especially true for those amputees who have no money to give themselves the best treatments. But here I am. Look at me. I have some resources and I am doing the best I can do by creating a community that is a safe space for amputees and also making them feel like they can make something out of their lives. Of course I am going back to medical school next year, but I would be going back with such a different personality and a different perspective about life and don't let me tell you that this doesn't scare me. It scares me as hell and I can only hope I keep having the strength to push and remain this strong person I have become. Trust me, it has taken a lot of work."

I could see it in her eyes that everything she was saying was true. She let me record her words. She said someday, I would know someone who would need those words. I hoped that I would be able to help someone with those words someday, just like she had said. My love for helping people was now second to none, to Diana's surprise. I loved helping people and I wanted to be the best at it. I felt like the whole thing was giving my life a direction, but I also did not want to think that I was thinking too much or I was only being too emotional because of all the people I was meeting. I wondered if I would feel the same way if I just made everything pause for a day.

CHAPTER EIGHT

When Mr. Andrews came around to our meeting to say there was an opportunity for some of us to go to Africa. I thought to myself, "an opportunity?" Who would want to go to Africa and not only that, feel like they had been done a favor by our support group booking their flight? Left to me, there were so many tourist attractions I'd rather visit all over the world and nowhere in Africa was exactly on my list, not even Cape Verde. At least not for now...all that would happen when I have visited Paris and other amazing places. In that moment, I was not even thinking about the fact that everything was supposed to be work-focused. It could never be me. I was super sure of this and I knew Mr. Andrew already knew this too and had probably factored me out. I say this because since I started volunteering, my mom has been very particular about my move, my meetings and everything else that involved my support group. According to my mother who keeps insisting that since she has lived far longer than me, there are many things she has experienced and heard of that I have never. So, based on that experience, many people could feign as support groups, NGOs and the likes with an ulterior motive. She had experienced many elections and general happenings in the United States of America to know that. The point is that she wanted her daughter to be safe. She usually talked about how she had seen people who originally planned to do good roped into horrible situations and she did not want that to be my case. I had everything I wanted. I had everything I actually needed to succeed in life; a great family, a bright future awaiting me (to be sponsored by my elder ones) and an amazing life in general ahead of me. She did not want that jeopardized by this one year of my life.

Hence, she had Mr. Andrew's number, she had Mrs. Martin's contact details too. She got the house addresses of each of them and this actually made me feel embarrassed because she had questioned their integrity to their faces. I know my mom; she did not mean to be a bad person. She just wanted them to know that someone was keeping tabs on them and if they tried to do anything that is not write with me or any of us, there was someone that was ready to trace them to the letter. Most of us that worked with them were youngins and my mom knew that. She had been to the office once during the six weeks of our training and once again during one of our meetings. To be honest, I felt embarrassed and I knew I could flare up like any random American kid would, but I understood her. The meaning of what she did actually ran deeper. If my father was alive, this was exactly what he would do, so she was just doing that too and I was not about to make her feel bad for doing that. Those two times she came, when she was leaving, I hugged her. She is a bit more cautious about me that Diana, in spite of the fact that we are age mates and I had only gotten involved in what Diana was doing before. This is the case because as my talks have connoted earlier, Diana is the one who acts more mature, so more was more comfortable leaving her to take care of herself. I was the more impulsive one, who jumps into things because I think they are exciting, so I definitely had to be checked. So, I don't blame her at all. However, sometimes, the whole thing is just funny to me because she had once said loosely that I was just like her when she was of my age. It was one of those days when we were driving to get a burger at night and I joked about her being too old for that. Then I saw a side of her that was just like me; a bit care-free about life and just wanting to experience everything without restrictions. Although my mom who was 5'7 tall and still wore a size 10 dress looked trim and fit, she knew how important it was to be careful about her diet as she grew older, but on that particular night, she did not care at all. Going back to what I said about her physique; yeah, that is very right. She has a great stature for a woman whose first child was 32 years old. She was only 54 years old anyway, but she looked 10 years younger. She is not one to joke with her skincare routine or spa sessions; you've just got to love my mom and maybe that is why when we go out together, she gets almost all the male attention and I get almost nothing. Very sad, right? Well, I guess I am still growing into everything I should be. I mean, I don't look bad myself, I got a lot of attention in high school and was close to being the prom queen if not for the fact that I did not care much about poise and I did not want my relationship to be public on that level. However, I don't look half as good as my mom, thanks to all those years of efforts she had put in to care for her body. My mom is a beautiful woman! Welp! Okay, I finally summarized everything I was trying to say; beautiful, not only in how she looked, but even how she talked and how she carried herself. One more confession from me: the way she looked was one of the reasons why I did not care that she barged into the support group sessions. She only made me look cooler and I did not mention earlier, but in the last week when she visited, I got many other teenagers who had just left high school also wanting to be my friend, because of my cool mom I guess.

And guess what? I turned them down! That's right! I mean, what do you think Beyonce would do? Haha! I'm only kidding. I sieved out two people I could actually hold as close friends and let go of some, while making some acquaintances. My mom's looks influenced my life that much and I guess that is why many people expected her to re-marry when my dad had died, but she chose not to. She decided to focus on her work and to be honest, I preferred that a whole lot. I was glad that I still had my mom to myself and I did not have to share her with some "Adam-specie" who would probably not understand the worth of the amazing woman that she is. Well, we're in the present and I am glad that my siblings and I only have to share her with work. So, let's just stop talking about the past for a moment.

However, sharing her with work isn't all perfect either. But please… it is definitely the better option. After my dad died, my mom requested for transfer to a department in her company that would require her to travel to several places in the world for work from time to time. Being a chartered accountant and being in that department was going to be a perfect distraction and create a new life for her as she had explained to my siblings and myself. She would travel to audit many big companies all over the world and auditing big firms took some time. So, she would be lodged in a hotel, sometimes alone and sometimes with her colleagues for some weeks (at least two weeks in most cases) and you can trust my mom to use that opportunity to see all the amazing sites in that destination for that period of time. She just kept having the time of her life and please, let's keep her beauty in mind, because it explains why this woman who is gunning for 60 years old is on Instagram! Not only that, but her page is cooler than mine because she has been to so many travel hotspots and everything is right there on her Instagram. And no, I did not set up that account for her. It was Diana that found out about the account when she was on a trip. We were surprised and at first, we felt like mom had crossed a line. She was already a blonde and had all the beauty, she could just leave Instagram for us, but she was there to stay. Apparently, an intern that worked under her had set it up for her and the one time I set my eyes on that girl, I gave her a hateful look. Nothing personal or maybe personal, because I would have loved to set up my mother's account by myself but I did not want her seeing on the shenanigans on my IG story. What seemed like the best thing to do was to block her, but how would I keep seeing her amazing pictures. I did not want to be told the tales by anyone else, especially my friends who adored her, had quickly found her and followed her on Instagram. So, here's what I did: I blocked her account, so she wouldn't see any of my activities and then opened a random account with no pictures and followed her to see her pictures. Luckily, I did so without those nosy investigators called my friends found out. I guess I was just lucky enough that they did find out about this move of mine all through high school days because they are quite good at this investigation thing. It was all fun back then too.

Then Mr. Andrew stopped at me and said, "You are doing such a good job at St. Greg's; you are one of the two people whose tickets we booked ahead, because we value you and we want to make sure you are coming with us." He had said this is low tones, and ended it with, "Let's keep this private for now." I could only smile and I smiled because I knew his game. I smiled because I knew what he was driving at and I was sure that there was no other person in the picture whose ticket had been booked. I was even sure that he had probably not even booked my ticket. He was just bluffing.

I guess you are now wondering why this 40-year-old man was bluffing about me coming to Africa. Well, it is about my mom. Maybe he didn't know that I noticed him hitting on my mom the two times she came around. When it comes to my mom, my antennas are always up. I usually know when someone is hitting on her and I knew Mr. Andrew only did this in an attempt to get at my mom. He wanted her calling him again and him having reasons to call her too. That way, they could start talking and maybe he could even invite her for lunch or something. This happens all the time or maybe I just watched too many movies. It was a bit weird to me to get used to people hitting on my mom, but I would not say it is not an achievable goal. You can totally get used to it. It is just that the feeling of giving them punches just never really leaves you. It just stays there and you just want to quickly do it while no one is watching with only both of you knowing that you had done it.

So, let's even talk about me. How do I even feel about the whole situation? One thing I have learnt in the course of volunteering is that even if nothing is wrong with you as a person, never neglect how you are feeling. No matter how you are feeling, you are feeling that way for a reason and running away from it does not solve anything. Most of the time, the best thing to do is to sit in how you feel and embrace the entire feeling until it is gone. That is how you get over feelings. Feelings are feelings; the truth is that they eventually fade, so whatever you are feeling is just for a while. This is something that has worked for many of the patients I see, especially when they are going through the stages of grief. They just have to sit in the feeling and embrace everything it is without trying to run from it. They have to go through the feeling that comes with each and every stage. Well, that's about that. I think I have gone too deep for what I want to talk about.

Honestly, I have grown to love helping people, but the whole Africa thing just seemed like a job to me. It is not like I don't like to help people in Africa, but it just seems so far away and the insurgency in some of the popular countries in the continent does not make me feel at peace to go there. Although in the past, I have talked about going to Africa to trace my roots, just like some of my other black friends have said, as my dad was black and my mom is white; now that it was right before my eyes, I did not just think I was ready for it. Yes, I could be impulsive, but not impulsive enough to go to a place that would make me fall sick altogether. I had to avoid what I could in the way I could.

However, Mr. Andrew wanted me to tell her anyway. She was going to be home in two days, and it was not even the type of news I wanted to break to her over the phone or a request I wanted to make to her over the phone. I had to play along for real because Mr. Andrew did not know about all the analysis I had done in my head. I just really had to play along. There was also a part of me that wanted to see where all this was going. I knew Mr. Andrew was headed for a heartbreak, I just liked to watch the process. However, it was a little bit shocking when I saw Mr. Andrew the next day at St. Greg saying that he had come by because he had been doing a routine supervision and he wanted to see how we were attending to the patients he was saying. He said this, but he spent more than half the time he was there only with my patients and I. Then at some point, he chipped in the talk about my mom. He commended me for being so dedicated and asked about if I had told my mom about the plans they had made for me. I tried to keep my reply as short as possible to avoid the conversation with this tall man who had celebrated his 40th birthday only two months ago and was actually well-built and handsome. In spite of being mixed, I am quite fond of black men and I just generally preferred them and Mr. Andrew was black, so maybe I was a little biased about his looks, but here's one thing I was sure of: he was not going to get my mother! Writing that felt very awkward…oops!

"No, I haven't" I said to him and I sensed that he wanted to ask more questions. Anyone else would have went on to say, "my mom is on a work trip, she's not back…" but definitely not me. I did not like to reveal too much details and I also really love the idea of suspense. I think it is the best thing that has happened to the movie industry and film-making in general.

"Oh. Alright." He seemed to swallow up all those questions of his. I was glad. I did not have the bandwidth for more discussions about my mom in that moment and I am sure that he did not want to make his intentions too obvious either. Win-win!

"I would see you around and keep up the good work." He said, after sitting with me and observing 10 more minutes of silence and nodding in approval to everything I did.

Mom got back the day after the next day and as usual, she wanted to go into her room and say little or nothing to anyone for the time being. As usual, she would soak herself into the bath tub once she was back, play some blues and sip her champagne. She had order Chinese and asked me to bring hers to her room once it was delivered. It was no time to talk to her about anything, so I just waited in silence for the suspense and how she was going to flare up about someone wanting her child to go back to Africa. I thought of how Mr. Andrew would then ask her to calm down and invite her over for lunch to talk. I wanted to see if she would turn him down or she wouldn't. so, since I knew that she would flare up, the first thing for me was to make sure that she rested as much as she wanted first. As for Mr. Andrew, I knew his game and knew that he actually had no choice, but to wait patiently for what happens next.

The only thing that bothered me about the whole process was that I hoped the Africa thing was not going to trigger any bad memory related to dad.

Africa and more precisely, the Lagos part of Nigeria was not as bad as the pictures usually connoted it to be. I'm talking about all those pictures with people always looking like they are about to die. I'm talking about those pictures with kids that are trying to get water from some stream with brown water to drink. Lagos, Nigeria was nothing like that. In fact, we were lodged in some hotel in a part of the city called Lekki and I could see many people driving good cars over there. They were living life normally too. There were many fun spots too and the night life in that area of the city looked amazing. I can say this for sure because we were stuck in traffic for a long time and when we started moving, it was at a snail's speed. It was a horrible thing to experience, but I was busy taking in the sights of the city, so it did not matter so much to me what was happening. However, at some point, it started to matter.

What I had not noticed about Lagos was what my friends that came along will later tell me about. And they did. I had fallen asleep from our time in the airport till when we got to the part of Lagos that was close to our hotel, so I had missed some parts of the city. Essentially, my friends were trying to tell me that not every part of Lagos was so amazing. While coming, we had passed some areas that were quite rowdy with kids hawking and some other things that showed that some of the pictures from Africa had been correct to an extent, but probably exaggerated, so whatever reason the creative that has showed the picture had in mind. It was an interesting place for a change. I felt excited to just have a different experience.

However, something was missing from this experience. I keep talking about "friends that came along to Africa", but they were more like acquaintances I had just had to work with and I had gotten really used to. The only real friend I had made from Helping Hands support group, Fiona, could not come with us even though she was also a very dedicated member. Something really sad had happened. Her dad had been diagnosed with prostate cancer, but she was not ready to give me the details just yet. I imagined it was really bad since she did not want to talk much about it for the time being. From experience, I also knew that people don't like to go into details of such so easy, especially not over the phone, because the last thing anyone in such a situation wants is pity. I had to let my friend be. I don't know if it was that she was truly busy or she was just avoiding me all that time before I travelled, but I understood that she might have really wanted to be alone until she had truly accepted the situation for what it is. She had told me her dad was not receiving treatment at St. Greg's and she would reach out when she was ready to talk. So, I had to let her be. Whenever we talked over the phone, she just wanted to talk about anything else aside her dad's situation. I had to let her go through her pain the way she wanted. It was the best thing to do. This was one year where I learnt that love meant staying away as much as it meant being with someone.

She had lost her mother so many years ago and her dad was her everything. Losing her mother was hard on her for years. She was the apple of her father's eyes; God forbid things got worse for him. Now, he had cancer and being his only child, my friend was definitely going to assume the role of the primary caregiver. That was no easy job and it hurt me that life had to happen that way. I wished she was with me, but I also knew it was a selfish thought. She had told me to have fun for two and send her pictures and videos. I had to toughen up and just do that for her. It will hurt her to know that I did not make memories she could view; I knew my friend. I just wondered how all those memories would be made since I did not have a friend to roll with. I did not exactly gel with people on a level where we can have fun like that together—selective me.

Anyway, bringing myself to my current sights, I was really looking to note some things that made Nigeria fall into the category of third world countries and I could really not wait to see. I knew the next couple of weeks will be interesting and I was really building up my interest.

However, I knew it would be more interesting with an amazing friend by my side.

There is a reason for which I was building my interest. I was building my interest because I never wanted to come at all, but my curiosity got me here. And I am not talking about my curiosity to come to Africa. I am talking about how curious I was to see what happens between my mom and Mr. Andrews. I could have found my way around making sure my mom and Mr. Andrew never met. I could have made an excuse that would make them never speak or simply say I was uninterested in the trip and leave the man with no choice but to try another way to get to my mom, which would have definitely been harder. I was just curious and generally wanted to see what his game was. I was sure his game was poor and he would get the shock of his life once my mom made him feel like he was not all that by putting him in his place. I could not wait to see this happen. I thought she would talk sternly about how she did not like that he was trying to get her attention through me and how I was not going to Africa for sure.

After I told mom that my ticket had been bought to travel to Nigeria in Africa. Of course, she flared up and said she really wanted to speak to whoever was in charge of the whole thing. She was really mad that anyone would do that without informing her because she still looked at me like I was only 17 years old. I guessed she just liked the feeling of having me to care for, so I was not going to take that for granted or make her feel awkward for feeling that way. I would have argued that I was 18 years old and was going on 19, but I really wanted to see how the whole drama would unfold. Yes! I was that curious. And please don't judge me. Looking back now, all I can say is that we all act foolishly at some point in our lives and that is okay. I was curious in a crazy way and it gave me what I was running away from. Turns out Mr. Andrew's game was tight. Maybe not tight enough to eventually get my mom, but tight enough to ensure I got on that flight. I figured that he was only bluffing, but that line of thought was wrong. When he went to see my mom, he really had soft copies of my ticket and he showed her. She was mad that he would do that, but he said it came as a gift from partners in Africa and he quickly thought of me as the best candidate. I knew that there were certainly no partners in Africa and he was such a liar. So, when mom told me that she had turned down the lunch offer and seen him in the office only to realize it was partners for Africa that sent the ticket, I felt like hissing. However, I took solace in the fact that he had bought my ticket with his own money (this I was sure of). The bad part was just the fact that mom had now made the entire story boring because of the way she had handled things. How could she be so straightforward? She should have played around with him for a bit, but I guess older women have no time for such games. Once they let you in, they really let you in and if they don't; well, sorry. As for my mom, I had not seen her let anyone in after dad died. This is why I was so confident about the whole Andrew situation. It was just painful that she had refused to infuse a bit of drama into the whole situation.

When I had brought up the issue of my support group wanting me to go to Africa, mom had talked so much of how she had been in Africa before and in fact many countries in Africa. She had talked about how she was scared about safety and everything else a mother would probably say to scare her child into not doing something. In the end, when she got back from meeting up with Mr. Andrew as she had chosen to in the office, she became more careful with her words. It was now about how Lagos was a fun place and she had been there for work. She talked about how she had made many friends and had even gotten invited to a Lagos party where there was a lot to eat and drink and how people just came in their different attires. I could just see that it was now a matter of convincing me to go. Mr. Andrew must have really gotten my mom to buy into the whole thing about partners getting me a ticket for my good work and how they would like me to come and help the volunteers in Lagos get motivated by reaching out to the patients they had been seeing. I knew this because she just kept talking about how proud she was of me and everything I had been doing. She talked about how I had grown so well even in her absence. It was really unlike her to talk like this, but I understood that this unnatural way of talking was definitely to ensure I got on that plane to Africa.

At this point, the curious cat in me had its mind changed from a "no" to "indifference" about the whole issue. I still felt like something more would come out of the situation because why else would Mr. Andrew still want me to come to Africa after mom had turned down his lunch. Why won't he just tell her he would make an excuse and fix in another volunteer for the opportunity. Why? I knew that the support group's financial unit will return the money he used to book the ticket, but that was quite a risk he took. What if I had decided that I was not going and not tole my mom at all? Well, the things men do...

I thought and thought that night. There had to be something else involved. Perhaps it was the fact that he knew that throughout the preparations and the trip, my mom would talk to me over and over. And I would be within his radius most of the time. Or the fact that at some point, she would probably have to talk to him about how I am faring. Well, in preparation for my trip, I had done a bit of research about Africa and comparing what I had seen to what I was now seeing in Lekki Lagos, a good job had not been done online or maybe I wasn't just looking in the right places. It could have also been the fundamental problem that there is already an underlying narrative about Africa that every report had to fit into or it was rendered useless. That was just really sad. Hence, I decided that I would do a documentary on my experiences while in Lagos, Nigeria. Nothing serious; just video clips I would post on my Instagram story and then collate in a place on my Instagram highlights. I was sure even my black friends now in college will be fascinated to see that there were actually some parts of Africa that were conducive for living and they could really visit without being so scared. There were bridges, there were water bodies, and beautiful cars. The grass was still green the same way it was in the United States and there was generally nothing to fear.

Getting to our hotel confirmed this even more. It was cozier than I ever thought it would be. We had the warmest people I have ever met of our age come around to welcome us. They promised to make our time in Lagos fun and I could only look forward to having all that fun because I needed enough videos to make my friends aware of how wrong we had been and the fact that some of the pictorial representations we had in our history classes were only a part of Africa or maybe the history we learnt just needed to be upgraded a little bit.

Mom had told me how she had been to Lagos and attended many parties. The next few weeks made me understand that a little better, because in spite of the stress they experienced on the road, it seemed like the people who lived in Lagos just wanted to enjoy life and everything in it. They loved to party a lot and that was not hidden in the way they behaved at hangouts. They would literally stand to dance to every song and you could always see the excitement in the air. Their music was also so dope. I liked them. I liked the people and how welcoming they were. I liked their vibe; it was everything and then some more. They believed in looking out for each other, they believed in caring for each other and it was just so normal among them. I noticed that they had different languages, but had English as their common language too. And oh, their accent. Their language affected it, but it was very sexy. I made so many videos and took many pictures. On my Instagram, my friends had so many questions for me. I had become their reporter in Africa. I basically attended to patients during the day and then, the evenings were for fun.

CHAPTER NINE

Lagos was actually a great city. I could see many people living great; having great standards of living. One of those days, as our bus drove me to report for duty, I saw some white kids in a school bus alongside the children of Nigerians. They were stuck in traffic, but I could see them relate with each other so well. At some point when the driver needed to adjust something and came down while in traffic to check the window, he rolled it down and then I could hear the kids speak. Their English was so fluent and they were all relating with each other really well, the white kids inclusive. It was such a beautiful sight to see. I wanted to capture it, but Mr. Andrew took my phone down and reminded me about the concept of privacy. Back at our hotel, we were also given the best treatment ever. The menu was so on point not because we were able to eat something we hadn't ate before, but because we had had English breakfast and everything was really proper; from the toast to the eggs to the bacon and everything else. I actually finished up every single portion of my meal, which is actually very unlike me. I am the kind of person that gets tired of food easily, but I did not get tired of the food, especially when they introduced me to their spicy jollof rice. I just kept eating non-stop. I took videos and I really wished I could learn the recipe.

People talked about Africa being rural and without basic amenities like water and electricity, but in this part of Lagos, none of these things was ever a problem. We had all the basic amenities. It appeared that we had been deceived over and over in the United States. Again, my curiosity made me find out what was happening from one of my new friends. They told me that this was true for some parts of Africa and Nigeria too. I was told that Nigeria was very big. She added that we were in a very sophisticated area of Lagos, so thinks were close to perfect.

For me, I only cared about the fact that there were parts of Africa where one could actually come to live and not experience anything scary as the media in the United States always portrayed. For at least five days after my arrival, I had not thought of the possibility of contracting any disease like they usually said once was likely to in Africa. It didn't cross my mind at all, because it felt like I was home and when you are home, you are comfortable and sure of hygiene, so it does not just cross your mind that you could contract any disease. This was really how comfortable I felt and I think the group in Lagos had done everything possible to make our stay perfect. I was especially falling in love with all the noise and happiness the night life in particular came with, but let's talk about that later.

My first patient was a breast cancer patient and she would rather be treated in her home in a part of Lagos called Ikoyi. Hence, I had to go to her home, but of course, I was taking all safety precautions. I also knew I was safe because our bus had dropped me there, so the entire group was there including Mr. Andrew. My mom had his address and knew his phone numbers. If anything went wrong with me, he would have to go back to the states and my mother would definitely have his head on a spike…just kidding!

Additionally, one of the volunteers in Lagos called Amaka had come with me. She used to be the one that attended to Mrs. Cole, but I was asked to show her how I did it by taking over for that week and just having her introduce me and then watching me and how I handled the patients. She had been friendly all along and it looked like working with her would be great. She was just as tall as I was and had very light skin. She was also really beautiful and had a nice smile to go with it. I knew we were in for a good time and she had even whispered something to me about going for lunch down the street if the bus delayed in the afternoon.

We walked in Mrs. Cole's home and if I could describe that place with one word, it would be "luxury". From the chandeliers to the painting on the wall, to the curtains and the glass table in the center of the guest living room, you could tell that everything used in setting up the home was of high quality and trust me: that does not come cheap at all. There were also helps dressed in white walking in and out of a particular room and going into another segment of the house at the far end of the guest living room.

"They are setting up breakfast for the family." Amaka whispered to me. I thought that was interesting, but I was now beginning to wonder where our patient was in all of these. A help had greeted us at the entrance. "Once we come in like this, it takes about twenty minutes to set her up for her session. That is what that help is now up to."

I had many questions for Amaka. The chief of them was why our patient wanted to talk to volunteers since she had enough money to employ the services of a psychologist, a counsellor or anything else she needed. Amaka began to narrate to me how the woman had been close to the private room of another patient in the oncology unit that was using the services of volunteers. Mrs. Cole had seen this and was just fascinated by the fact that the volunteers were so young. All her kids were grown and had moved out of the country, yet she really liked having young people around her, hence she requested to have volunteers come talk to her. The first volunteer that worked with her kept talking about how fun and lively the woman was. She was not hopeless. She was excited to be alive and getting little things she wanted like this. Obviously, there was so much more to her. Eventually, she left the hospital and decided that she would get home care when things got better with her health. Hence, she had a room in her home set up like a standard private room in the oncology unit. She employed the services of healthcare professionals to also come see her on shifts as she was not one to joke with her health in the least bit. The volunteer that was seeing her also got involved in other personal engagements and could not continue. Hence, Amaka was asked to step up to the role and so she did.

The helps were still setting up breakfast and then one of them came to invite the girls to the table, but I declined. I had enough back in the hotel. Amaka on the other hand was going to join them at the table. Well, it was just Mr. Cole and one of the Cole nephews that had come around. I knew it would have been awkward if I said no when my friend was going to eat.

"They are cool people." Amaka whispered to me. "...and trust me, they always insist that I join them whenever I come in at a time they're about to eat."

We walked towards the dining room and I realized that the sitting room had been bigger than what I previously thought. The mirrors on the wall made things a bit confusing. Well, I walked down the room to get to the door that led to the dining room.

"We thought it was nice that you ladies should join us while they get done with the setting up." Said Mr. Cole with his Nigerian accent that was quite glaring.

"Of course, Mr. Cole. Good morning." Said Amaka.

"Good morning Mr. Cole." I said.

He stared at me for a moment and then said, "Oh, one of the volunteers from the state. It's a pleasure to meet you." He dug for more eggs. I had only tea. Amaka had tea and some toast. The breakfast was such a full table, too full for four people, even ten. It was later on that Amaka told me that Mrs. Cole did not joke with feeding her family with excess and even cancer could not stop that. It just had to be a full table and the helps as well as the chefs, knew what it had to be and they followed suit with how they made the food and arranged the table. I imagined that these people were quite wealthy, as they definitely lived like royalty. Amaka and I actually had the breakfast more of in silence, nodding here and there and giggle when appropriate. All the while, we gave each other the side eye as if to confirm how to react to each situation before reacting. Just imagine the way you would act when your best friend introduces you to strangers and you are trying to act right. Yes, that explains the way we were acting. It actually felt like I had known Amaka for longer or maybe I had just assumed that teenagers and young adults in Africa wouldn't be as sophisticated or know little sign languages like the side-eye thing. Well, it turns out that I was very wrong and I actually knew nothing about Africa or its people. I was just happy that I was discovering something new. My imagination was now really broadened. I could imagine what it was like to have so many parts of Africa with different languages, cultures, and standards of living. If I had not travelled, I would probably not be thinking this way, as my view about life would be so limited. In fact, if someone else had told me this and that about travelling to Africa, I wouldn't have all the understanding I now had in that moment. I guess that is what they say about travelling; travelling gives you a different world view by taking you out of your bubble where you think life starts and ends.

Life does not start and end in your bubble. There is so much that humans would only realize if you mix with other humans in another part of the world. Social media does not even come close in narrating these experiences to you at all. In all, I was grateful that I had come. I was no longer indifferent. I was glad I had come and I could see why mom decided to take a role that would make her travel more after dad's death. It did a lot more for her. It made her happier and probably created a new life or the possibility of one for her. I can say this because all the while being in Africa, I had hardly remembered my life in the United States or missed it. All I cared about was what the possibilities were the next day; not what had happened in my past. I had travelled to a few tourist attractions, but travelling to a place that holds a lot of history that is perhaps tied to you hit a lot differently. So, I am not saying everywhere mom travelled gave her the effect I talked about, but specific places probably gave her that. Being where I was felt like a different world and seeing people just like me being so amazing and living their best lives felt good too. Now, I was somewhere that really felt like a castle (but without towers) and I was seeing that there were people who woke up to luxury in Africa too and were not thinking of rushing to get to work before 8.a.m.

"Oh! It's nice to meet you." Said Mrs. Cole as I stepped in just behind Amaka.

"You are pretty and hope you like Nigeria."

"Yes, I do." I replied with a smile.

I had not been expecting that level of energy from Mrs. Cole, to be very honest. I was a bit blown away by the way she welcomed me. She had such a lively spirit that I had wondered where all that energy came from.

"Nice to meet you ma'am."

From the way she was talking, I knew that she really just needed people to chat with. It looked like she had moved on from her situation and she was not depressed in anyway. Perhaps, chatting was her own way of coping with the whole situation; seeing young ones like us and just chatting. She was watching an amazing US TV series by the time I went in. I thought to myself that this woman really had no worries whatsoever. It was amazing to see that she was really carrying on with her life after her the mastectomy of her right breast. She had swelling in her right arm which was not a strange sight after mastectomy, but a physical therapist was also seeing her to control and reduce that swelling in her arm. I looked from her and to the TV. Amaka just sat there, unbothered and watched TV with Mrs. Cole too.

Then she paused the TV as she was quick to notice my confusion.

"I used to be one of the writers of this particular television series. I like to watch previous episodes every morning. It just takes me back to those times when I used to wake up to write first thing in the morning because that was when the plot ideas flowed best for me. You know, rising early before anyone else rises and tuning into the frequency of the morning gives you a kind of energy that is hard to get at any other time of the day."

I was in awe. "Ma'am, so you were really one of the writer. That is so amazing. This remains one of my best series ever. Wow! I am sitting with a celebrity, I said." She went on to show me her name as one of the writers, as the crew was on display at the end of each episode. "Grace Cole" was her name and for this reason, no one would imagine that she was from Africa. She talked about how if she had imagined it would be like that, then she would have used her native name—"Funmi Cole" for a proper representation of Africa. Hence, it dawned on me that not only were some parts of Africa very habitable for people from some parts of the world. There were very smart people in the African community too—smart enough to land a gig that many people whp lived in the United States could not land.

It was a proud moment for even me, knowing that this woman had achieved that. Her husband had also established businesses all over the world, so they could afford to live like royalty, especially now in their relatively old age when their two kids were now married and all they had was each other.

The remaining part of the session consisted of our patient calling in the help to bring her pictures from the past. There were several albums and she was sure to show me those when she had gone to sign her deal for the gig in London. All I could think of was the fact that she must have been really good at what she did for her to be able to rise to that height by merely sending an entry via an email.

"The painful thing is that the only part of my life that has been grossly affected by cancer is my creative juices. To be honest, it is more like I spend all my energy on trying to be so positive and chase away whatever negative thoughts that want to come my way. For this reason, I have no strength whatsoever left to be creative too. I always feel drained once it is time to write. Hence, after working on that series for the last eight years, I decided that I would take a break from it, so I don't destroy the good legacy I have created by submitting subpar work. However, it gives me so much joy to watch what we have done in the past. It is beautiful to see that it is an interesting series. While I was actively writing, I hardly watched. It made me cringe or brought me to tears the few times I watched and saw a scene that was based on what I wrote, as there were also other writers on the team."

She explained that it was like watching her part of her on TV. She explained that her writing felt like a part of her and watching was just too weird for her.

"I miss writing. I miss letting the world see a very important of me. You know, a lot of things go on in my brain and being able to put them in writing just makes me feel better. However, now, I would rather talk than write. Yet, there is so much that goes on in my brain. I can't just sit down to do it. Maybe this feeling actually stems from the fact that I feel like a writer should be a perfect person. A writer should be without blemish. On a subconscious level, this is how I feel. Because art must be given in a raw manner to the world. Art does not deserve to be adulterated in any way. And my body is not perfect anymore."

"What if you create a different meaning for perfection?" I asked. Our session had indeed begun. "What if you redefined what we should call perfection?"

It appeared she loved my mind and how I reasoned. I could understand that, especially based off the fact that she was a writer.

"There's nothing better than a dynamic mind!" she exclaimed in adoration. Amaka also cheered. What they did not know yet was that I had more practical ideas; a solution to the fact that the patient we had been talking to could not do what she loved to do and knew how to do so well in the moment. I believed that her healing would be accelerated if she felt like she was doing some good in our fallen world, by sharing some of her amazing ideas with everyone and perhaps the company she had struck her deal with. After all, she had only gone on a break to care for health and during that break, she had gotten a chance to watch the movies. She had paid attention to the movies by watching as an outsider.

She had now seen the loopholes and she was just the one in the best position to fix them.

I had just the perfect solution for her to share those ideas, but I kept wondering if she had thought of those ideas in the past and just realized that they would not work for her. I hoped my idea would be a fresh one and I hoped that even if she did not use it, she would at least thrilled by my idea. That was all I was really asking for. Anyway, I decided to blurt it out without thinking too much and just see where it would lead.

"Ma'am, I think you can equally share your ideas by recording them as opposed to writing. And while I agree with the fact that writing really helps in organizing thoughts and reaching to parts of your heart you never knew existed, recording also brought out an amazing part of you. Recording would reveal undiluted truths in my own opinion. Although both methods are different and may not bring the same results through and through, at least you would not let this sickness win over your creativity. Who knows? You could possibly pick up after recording for a while. I would really like you to give this a try ma'am."

I stopped talking and then realized that I had been talking for quite a while. This had been the case because she had been nodding in affirmation to everything I was saying all along. She seemed impressed by my little TED talk. However, there was still a brief moment of silence.

When she eventually spoke, she said, "thank you for the great idea. I am happy to have such a great suggestion, as I have waited for one for a long time. It is funny how this is not farfetched yet brilliant. I am thrilled!"

Funnily, she had never thought about the idea of recording at all. I had just thought it up in that moment too. Honestly, I had impressed myself too. It felt like my yearning to help others was bringing out parts of me that I never knew existed.

That evening, we stayed in the lounge of our hotel and had fun getting to know a bit more about each other. Honestly, it was more like most of us from the states trying to understand more about Africa. Because those in Africa seemed to know more about America than we that live there know. I cannot say that I was not fascinated by that level of knowledge and dedication.

It is sad as I cannot say the same for us. We were just too busy trying to know the parts of Africa where humans and wildlife really lived together. As we looked around and asked, it was awkward to even us. I mean, we had been all over Lagos. How did we even dare to still ask that kind of question? It was definitely the wrong type of question to ask after everything we had seen and after how much we had socialized with them. Most of us could agree that in that moment, we had been wrong to think like that because it is inhumane to think that anyone at all would live with animals. In that moment, we realized that it was impossible for that to happen and it was really an insult to the people in question. We were really sorry; not just for our question, but for our way of thinking for almost as long as most of us lived. We had taken in what we had heard, but we now also knew that it was on us to educate others that those beliefs were very wrong and such things should never be said about our fellow humans anymore. The fact that our beliefs can be centered on nasty jokes got me in awe and I was more in awe about how those nasty jokes had even grown to become our truth.

As we went on with the night, a call came in for Amaka.

"Mrs. Cole" she whispered to me as she excused herself to take the call. We had quite taken to each other within our few days of working together and I had definitely grown to love her so much. She was the best buddy ever and she was sophisticated enough for me to make jokes about my escapades in the states to her. She was very much a traveler herself and had been in New York twice. I could not help but gist everyone back at home about my new friend up to the point that I was sure that they were probably tired of hearing about her all the time. The next thing on the itinerary should have been meeting her if not that we were in fact halfway across the world. When I saw her walking into the longue with a big smile plastered across her face, I could bet that it was some exciting news and yes, I was right.

It was Mrs. Cole on the phone and I wondered why she would be calling at that time. It was Thursday and we had been seeing her every day that week since Monday.

"She has set up a fun weekend for us with her nephew." Amaka said as she almost leaped for joy.

On my part, I liked to have fun, but I also thought it to be a dicey situation. "Are we supposed to be getting close to patients up to this level?" I asked.

"Well, she said she would call in our favor, so you have absolutely nothing to worry about aside the outfits you are going to wear for the various activities they have planned out for us.

Amaka went on to tell me how Mrs. Cole had set up several activities for us to have fun at major areas in the city of Lagos from the afternoon of the next day, which happened to be a Friday, and throughout the weekend. She went on to say how she was particular about me having all the fun the city had to offer, so I would have enough tales to tell when I was back home. The things that excited me the most was the fact that we were going to be kayaking and going on a boat cruise. Amaka had also mentioned to me how we would be visiting various restaurants and all would be on Mrs. Cole's account. I really needed someone to wake me up at that point and tell me I was dreaming because if anyone had told me at the beginning of the year that I would be living my best life and meeting the best people somewhere across the world on another person's account, I would have looked that person in the face and called that person a liar. However, this was my reality at this point and if you are looking for a living proof of such miracles, dear reader, you have every cause to look at me for sure.

Mrs. Cole apparently had great influence. The next day, the man in charge called Amaka and I. He told us that we were free to go have fun as Mrs. Cole had called in our favor and had assured them that our safety was really guaranteed. I looked Amaka in the face and realized that I was the only one who was surprised. The day at Mrs. Cole's house was quite a chatty one that day. She had one of the helps serve as strawberry tea and cookies. Whenever tea was served, I knew for sure that the chat was probably going to be a long one. Anyway, it was Mrs. Cole and she was always fun, so I was ready. Well, so I thought, but I was really not ready for the amazing ride down the story lane which she eventually took us through.

"Girls, I want you to live your life while you can and do it unapologetically." She started. Amaka and I looked at each other, apparently wondering what was up with her intensity on that particular day. She was being quite intense.

"Well, I said unapologetically, but of course without causing any damage to your future, okay?" We nodded in agreement.

"What you don't want is to have any permanent dent of any sort on your life." She paused again. "In my days, I could say I had fun, visiting the best of places and meeting the best people without caring too much. Of course, I took my education seriously and I built my writing skills as I have always loved to write. However, I took fun seriously too. Trust me, memories from those times are part of what keep going now. The fact that I can look back and actually say I had fun makes me so happy. I literally lived my best life without knowing that any sickness was coming my way. As I took life seriously, I did not joke with the concept of enjoying life and all it brought too. That is why I am not so sad about the turn of events in my life; trust me, I am not as sad as I would be if in those days, I had no fun and visited no place. Just imagine me saying I would do things later and now that my body is moving differently, I cannot do them anymore. Can you imagine the level of frustration that could bring my way? That is why I decided to organize that trip for you girls. Trust me, it is not even about me helping you, you are also helping me. I want to relive those days by seeing you have fun." She concluded.

Being the American that I am, I moved closer to hug her the best way I could.

"No, you don't have to do that." she giggled, as she beckoned on me to stay off. "I just need you to take amazing pictures for me. That's what I really want."

"We would take so many pictures." Amaka said and I nodded in agreement. That was the last time we were going to have an official visit to her place, but she asked that we both come back to see her, especially before I left.

We had so much fun for the rest of the weekend and I did not even want the weekend to come to an end. We were also sure to take enough pictures for every event for Mrs. Cole. Of course, I paid her one more visit before I left Nigeria and it was quite an amazing one. I love that woman and she is definitely amazing.

My experience with Mrs. Cole just made me realize that there was a broad range of people going through similar experiences irrespective of their socio-economic, social and political classes. And all of them had different stories and different things they needed to heal from. Yet, their sickness remained a common point for all of them.

There was something else that made me drawn to Mrs. Cole. I had not noticed, but I was quite drawn to her vibe and I didn't even notice how I was very excited to always see her until one day when Amaka called my attention to it.

"Gabby, you are usually more excited than usual to see Mrs. Cole." She had said.

"Oh, really? I don't think so." I said, but I had also caught myself in the act at that moment. It was at that point that I knew that being with her had triggered a happy memory from my past. That night, I stayed up in my hotel room, staring at the ceiling and wondering what it was it. Gradually, the memory I had buried started coming back to me. I had buried the memory because it was a good one that ended very badly.

The first time I lost anyone, it was my grandmother. She had died a few years before my dad and it hurt little me so much when my mom told me that my grandma had gone to become an angel and I knew that angels did not live on earth. I wanted my grandmother to live with us. I wanted her to live on the earth. However, being an angel was supposedly a good thing, so I had no right to say what I truly wanted. I wanted my grandma to live on the earth and not as angel. I loved her so much.

Times with her were gold. She always read me stories and bought me ice cream. She combed my hair and always told me that I was beautiful. I just loved her so much. She had Mrs. Cole's kind of vibe; never sad in spite of the fact that she spent her last year of being alive in the hospital.

It was when I was in final year of my senior high that I developed the courage to ask my mom what actually happened to her. It was then that my mom told me that they only discovered that granny had breast cancer when the disease was at its final stage. Apparently, she had been asking very strong and like everything was fine with her in spite of the fact that she had been experiencing symptoms and severe pains for a long while. All that time, she was still being the same source of joy to everyone. It was just funny to me how she and Mrs. Cole had the same condition and they were very alike too. It is so funny how people that were seas apart from each other in this world could be so similar to each other. I laughed hard when I finally realized what it was. Perhaps Mrs. Cole was granny's gift to me. I hadn't even realized that the little girl in me still missed my granny that much. From the moment, I did not hide the way I felt anymore. I embraced how I felt each time I had any contact whatsoever with the woman.

CHAPTER TEN

Amaka and I were going to be a pair throughout my time in Nigeria and I really liked that. She was dedicated yet fun-loving just like myself, so she was my perfect match. I cannot even begin to narrate our several escapades after our sessions in the second week. I had so many memories already in the second week and many sights in Lagos to remember when I was gone. It was already apparent to me that I would miss Lagos when all was over. And we were only in the second week when I started feeling this way. However, I would like to talk more about our third week.

We were assigned to a lady with skin cancer. She was only 23 years old and the crazy part was the fact that she was a model. She had modeled for several brands because of her amazing skin as well as her grooming, but now, here she was, suffering from skin cancer and having a hard time doing any campaign for any brand. This was not only based on the reactions her skin was prone to having, but based on the fact that she did not feel good in her own skin anymore.

On getting to house on Victoria Island, where she lived with her staff (help, cook, security and driver), I was amazed to see that a model in Africa who was only 23 years old was doing so well. She was getting the kind of treatment the models across the globe would get too. Then,

I quickly remembered that she was working with global brands and getting paid in foreign currency. What I had noted about Nigeria was the fact that my US Dollars were worth quite more here, so it was not hard to process the fact that she was living like a queen because she was earning so much in foreign currency. All the staff treated us with so much respect as we walked into her home. It was a duplex with two bedrooms upstairs and I wondered why she was living there all alone. I later got to know that she preferred to live alone because she wanted privacy for her relationship and she also hosted her foreign friends that were models from all over the world whenever they had anything to do in Nigeria and in fact, they usually used her home for a mini-party or to just have some private girl time as they could ensure that no man would come except they let him in, as it was no public place. Hadiza was really a cool one and Amaka explained to me that she was from a northern part of Nigeria known as Fulani. Their females were known to be tall and very beautiful. They were also the lighter skinned women for blacks. On meeting Hadiza, she fit perfectly into the description. She was a popular model, so Amaka was just happy that she was getting to meet her and hoping that she could be her friend. I was sure to remind her that a move like that was not exactly permitted when it came to the patients we dealt with.

We talked to them about very private matters, hence, we were expected to dissociate ourselves from them when our time with them was over. Any relation with them in the next five years following our time with them was considered unethical.

"Of course, I know." Amaka replied me. "If only wishes were horses…" she said. I could understand her.

When we got in, the help ushered us into her room as she said Hadiza had instructed. However, when we got into the room, all we could here was sobs from somewhere within. Out of curiosity, I walked in and around. I was wondering what might have happened. Perhaps, someone had broke in or something. I was actually scared that she was in danger.

"The sobs are coming from there." Amaka pointed in the direction of the closet. Hadiza had to be in a corner of the closet. We were still looking at each other and wondering the best approach to talk to Hadiza for a start when we heard footsteps. She must have heard Amaka's voice when she talked about the sobs coming from the closet. To be honest, those sobs had been very faint. The room was quite a big one, but it had been extra quiet when we came in; quiet enough for the sobs to have been heard.

"Hey! Hi" I guess you are from the support group. It was at this point that I wondered why Hadiza had decided to use the support group since she could afford therapy. It was later on that I got to know that she had opted to use the support group because she had been involved in a lot of media drama, right up to the point that she had caught her last therapist in bed with her ex and it had gone really viral. She currently happened to be at a point in her life where she really needed people she could trust, but was not even sure that she had any. She only had a few friends and one of them happened to be a director of the big and influential Lagos support group and had sworn to keep her secret safe. She had not let the brands know about her cancer, as she knew it could lead to an immediate termination. She could hardly tell anyone anything because each time she left her house, she had to put on a persona that fit into who people believed she should be and how they believed she should act. Her celebrity friends did not make things any easier for her. It was not like they were doing anything wrong. They were not just the best for her at the moment, as everyone in the show biz is always really about show biz and getting hard core friends had always been a problem. Now, she just wanted regular people that she could talk to.

"I was just trying to check out my clothes in the closet. I was looking through for those that still fit properly. I have just lost a lot of weight of recent."

"Oh, that's interesting. We could help look through and see which still fits like it should, if you want us to." Amaka said, in spite of the fact that we could see that her eyes were clearly red and swollen. Playing along was really important at this phase as it was obvious that Hadiza wasn't rather to talk about the actual issue. It was understandable and no matter how the concept of a support group made it look, we were still very much strangers who Hadiza was trying to get used to. I saw the way she looked at me when you came in.

"You're not from Nigeria, right? You seem like you just came in." she said, as we organized the clothes in color.

"Obvious much?" I asked.

"A bit. Your accent gives you away too."

"Haha! That's a pity for me. I was hoping I could camouflage as one of you."

"Mission aborted my dear." She said.

I was happy that we could pick up from somewhere. She seemed to be a good conversationalist, but that was expected of her, considering her line of work. Anyway, we were off to a good staff and we spent yet another hour talking about clothing brands, high street fashion and anything else you would expect female young adults to discuss about fashion. She knew quite a lot of things about the fashion industry of the United States and revealed to us that she had been taken fashion school classes online. She was even looking to start up a clothing line soon, but she added that this was privileged information and she had only mentioned it because we had been talking a lot about fashion. It was obvious that this was indeed an industrious young lady that had many plans in her head. She was not just another lady with a beautiful face or a perfect body. She talked about the fluctuations in the market and fall of the Nigeria currency, naira, against the dollar and how it could really affect her prices which she had really wanted to be affordable to the girl-next-door who wanted to be elegant. This is because the quality of material and other things she needed to make the wears needed to be imported from all over the world. I engaged her saying I had expected that I expected that she would want to make clothes for celebrities since she was very much one of them and it would probably be easier for her to make sales among them, even at high prices. I really wondered why she had chosen to make clothes for the average lady because it would be a factor her branding and a great determinant for her price. I had seen my elder sister shop from different brands and I could say that some clothes did not match their prices; it was just their branding that made them worth more.

"I understand this business, my dear." She started. "However, I am not from a wealthy background. I had a very humble upbringing, but I had always wanted to be a model. I found that I needed to go for many auditions and attend many events and little things like the brand I wore for those occasions were what were bound to make me stand out. I could not afford the kind of clothes I needed to wear because they were not designed with the interest of people like me at heart. They were designed for celebrities, they were designed for the rich and there were no clothes designed for people like me. Maybe clothes from brands like Zara would have been affordable enough for me, but thanks to the charges on importation and the profit the sellers had to make, those clothes ended up being just as expensive as the clothes I could not afford. Things were really tough for me in the beginning and I just want to open the door in the way I can for those coming behind me. I may not be able to give them all modeling gigs, jobs or anything else. They may not even be in my field. They may be trying to climb the corporate ladder. I want to help such ladies with my brand and that is what this is about for me."

I was about to give her a round of applause, but Amaka was already doing it. We all burst out into laughter as she clapped. Honestly, if that was a speech to cart away the Miss. U.S.A crown, she was probably going to win that crown. I was moved by the fact that she was a kind person and climbing so high had not changed that for her. It was very beautiful to watch and I was inspired by all her virtues. She was really a grounded person and didn't deserve cancer messing up her career in any way. She deserved better from life, but we could not give that to her. We could just do what we could to ensure she has proper support. We had to step into the shoes of real friends for her. She was really trying to keep her condition out of the eyes of the public. She had a treatment room set up for her at home and a private doctor coming to see her under the highest level of privacy and security. She definitely had to be paying hugely for that. It was a sure thing. It was stage two skin cancer and although she had been scheduled for surgery, her doctor just came in for the time being for general check-up and to be sure that there was nothing she was doing that was going to make the situation worse. This is why she also needed to talk to people who felt like friends, at least because the time before surgery is when acceptance of the condition has to be settled with the patient, and that's pretty hard to achieve.

Amaka walked to the other side of the closet where Hadiza was seated. It was quite a big closet and could probably make a small room for another person. "It's been amazing being here with you Hadiza. It is nice to know that your smiles on all those billboards come from such a beautiful heart." She paused and the silence in the room in that moment was deafening. She placed her hand on Hadiza's shoulder and asked, "But how are you Hadiza?"

Hadiza paused and looked around. She stood up and paced. I could feel the energy in the room somewhat jerking up as she paced. I knew moments like that. I recognized it. I knew that when she talked, it would be truly from her heart.

"Well, I am scared!" she said, and then burst into tears. I was going to rush to her side and embrace her in my arms, but she gestured to me not to come. She wiped her tears and just kept talking. "I am scared that I would have to let down everyone depending on me. I would have to let down all those mouths that depend on me to feed. I would have to let down everyone that looks up to me as a beacon of hope. How does someone climb so high, yet have a sickness they did not bargain for come pull down everything they had worked for? I did nothing to deserve this. I never joked with my skin or used anything harsh on it. However, I am not even bothered about myself, I am more concerned about all the promises I may not be able to keep to the people I love. This might really affect my career and I don't care about if they say it's just the second stage and all I would need is surgery. Things don't always work that way. Surgeries could really go wrong; anything could happen and my career would come to such an end. I don't want to even imagine it, because if my career is dead, even my fashion plans may go to ruins. It scares me to think about the future. I wish I was not reasoning like this, but I can't even help it."

To crown it all, she could not even tell her family all of what was going on with her. Her three younger ones depended on her for their education and were already doing quite well with their studies. She did not want their hopes to come to nothing on knowing that their sister might not be able to afford to sponsor their education anymore. Her father had stroke and was paying hugely for physical therapy and several other consultations. She had also promised to set up her mother's business on a larger scale, but was currently directing the funds she was supposed to use for that into her healthcare and for all the preparations for her surgery. It was almost like she regretted having to touch that money. As she spoke, I could see it in her eyes.

"You blame yourself." I said. "Stop blaming yourself. It would be horrible for all these to happen to you or your family, but if you do not live up to anyone's expectation because of some situation that is out of your control, it is not your fault." I told her.

That's the thing about counselling. Many people would assume that it means I had to tell her sweet nothings that would cheer her up, but that was not the best. The patient actually needs to sit with the truth and keep every possibility in mind, while focus on the most positive ones. If this is not the case, if there are unrealistic expectations and things do not go as planned, then you would end up having to deal with a worse situation, another breakdown from the patient and it would be like starting all over; starting from square one to bring the cancer's patient mind to a positive place. At this point, many patients could even give up on themselves and just think that there is nothing good that could ever come out of their situation again. And that is not a good thing.

"Thank you so much." She said. "I am glad to have been able to talk to you about this. It has been weighing heavily on my mind and it is funny how in some situations, it is best to talk to people who are seemingly strangers and do not know so much about you."

We spent the rest of our time there doing something Hadiza loved to do. Really, it felt better around her this time, and she kept talking about how she actually felt like a heavy weight had been taken off her neck. She was free as a bird, arguing about the scores on each game. I found it a bit weird that she liked to play games though, but she said she had just been fortunate to be with male counterparts from time to time and had no choice but to learn to play a couple of games.

We also made cookies and when it was time to leave that day, we felt like we had spent ages in the house. It was quite a memorable one and we already felt like friends. She kept saying she wished we could sleepover, but for privacy policies and all that, we had to go for sure.

I spent most of my night thinking about our day with Hadiza and could not wait to see what would happen for the rest of the week. We already felt like friends, but I remembered the policy that said we could not stay friends for years. Then, I looked it up again to see, only to realize that we could be friends if it was the patient's will. That even justifies the fact that Amaka and I still had direct contact with Mrs. Cole and she had still chatted each of us up that morning. It was on her terms; she obviously wanted to keep the relationship…amazing!

We resumed at our point of duty the next day honestly thinking that it would be one of those days when we would be able to have fun and just enjoy our girl time with Hadiza without caring about the rest of the world. We were going to make her feel like a badass who can go through anything too. We had thought of how we would keep reminding her of all her accolades, how she had started from the scratch to get them and how it was a pure indicator that she could do absolutely anything she set her mind upon. I guess that was a cute plan, a really cute one. However, it seemed like the universe had a different plan for us that day.

It really ended up being one of those days that just made you question everything about people.

We got to the house and the help said Hadiza had asked us to only stay in the living room once we were in. This was strange and we whispered to each other, wondering there was something we had done wrong the previous day. Perhaps we laughed too much or she just realized that we had crossed her boundaries too easily, and she just needed a break before she could trust us again. Anyway, we sat there wondering and waiting for Hadiza to come out and clear our doubts or re-emphasize our worries.

We waited for another twenty minutes and while we stared at the television, anxiety was actually eating us up big time. It was really hard to concentrate on anything else aside our worry. The worry had even shifted to the question of if she was actually doing okay. After those twenty minutes, the help came to tell us to come in. By the time we were in, we said our greetings but instead of responding, Hadiza ran to us, held us both tight, then moved her head totally to Amaka's right shoulder and burst into tears. It was what you would refer to as a loud cry and Amaka and I stared at each other wondering what happened to her. Amaka held her close, while I patted her on the back still wondering what had happened, yet trying to calm her down. I was just hoping that her cancer had not gotten worse or anything. I just kept wondering what could make her cry so hard. Maybe her cancer story had been released to the public or maybe she had lost a huge deal already. Many things were just running through my mind and none of the scenarios I thought of was better than the other.

"He's engaged!" she finally said. "He called her his friend and now they are engaged." She paused and looked at the both of us who were even more confused. "What are you talking about?" I asked, staring at her. She only pulled out her phone and showed me a proposal video of a couple that looked really cute and of course, I did not recognize them. Amaka leaned in to look.

"I did not know this footballer was dating this ex-beauty queen. How did that get past everyone?" she asked.

"There's so much that nobody knows! There's so much that gets past the media—like the fact that I was the one he was dating all along while he always called her his long-term friend. Why would he do this to me? I don't deserve this and not even at this time of my life." She cried.

"Oh! I'm so sorry." I said as I hugged her. I mean, I know of 1001 horrible ways to breakup with someone, but a public proposal to a different girl and a popular figure at that, tops it all. He was a horrible person to have done that to her.

She narrated the entire thing to us. He had said he was going to sign a deal in Paris and he was going to be there for a while. He had been there when it was confirmed that she had skin cancer, but she had decided to stall until he was back and she could talk him in person. Right up to the night before the proposal, they had been talking on facetime. A heartbreak like that was just something else. I could only wonder how he had managed to pull off talking to her regular yet being on a staycation with someone else, up to the extent of proposing. It was the craziest thing I have heard of when it came to breakups.

Apparently, since they were public figures, they had decided to keep their relationship very private until they got engaged or even right up to the point of their marriage. It was a dream for them to take the entire media by surprise, only for this to happen with his ex-beauty queen that he referred to as his long-term friend. Although in her one year of dating this footballer that hailed from Nigeria, but played for a club in the UK, she recalls meeting this ex-beauty queen based in the UK only twice and in those times, they were reportedly cool with each other. She was beyond heartbroken, her heart had been shattered and it was not even the right time for that to happen to her.

"Why not me? Why didn't he propose to me?" she kept asking. I could see that the whole situation was already making her feel like there was something wrong with her. And as much as I wanted to tell her that there was nothing wrong with her, I also knew that there was a time to talk and a time to be quiet.

The fact that we were only one week away from her surgery when this horrible news broke in was too bad. Her management had to step in by bringing in an assistant to her house who was going to be with her phone and attend to anything from the media at all. She was not to have any contact with her phone for the time being, except it was family of course. I saw the sweet Hadiza go from sad about her sickness to worrying about what blogs were carrying as she had already seen pictures of she and her ex all over the internet with all forms of captions and shades before her phone had been taken away from her at all. There were rumors all along as to if they were dating as they had been spotted in some places together but they had always done a good job in getting past the news. Now, all those pictures were resurfacing on the internet and there were rumors of the truth about what had happened and how he had really ditched her. She had seen all these and her management had seen everything too. That is why they stepped in to help. In spite of the new assistant staying with her round the clock, Hadiza still insisted on having us stay with her too. She had called to request that from the coordinator in Lagos and we had been given the go-ahead to stay there if we wanted to. To be honest, it was quite glaring that she needed all that support from us. She had lost weight in a few days and with her surgery coming up, she really needed all the strength that she could get. She needed to be happy for the time being and although making her truly happy from within was probably not very achievable within the short while, at least, we knew that we could get her to just feel better by doing things that would light up her mood. There were lots of series and since she could not go out or do anything strenuous for the time being, at least we could play virtual reality games to take her somewhat out of the house and I could see that for whatever five minutes she had to play virtual reality games, she was happy. She was taken away from her need to worry or stress about some man that never deserved her or even the lady he was now proposed to. He must have been lying to that lady about Hadiza and if that lady knew that he was fooling Hadiza and just played along, she was also a fool. He was definitely not a man that would stay faithful to her. I wish Hadiza could see the bright side to the whole situation which I was seeing for her. A new chapter of her life was about to open and she did not even know it. I could see that coming for her. All these things happening to her had to so those new doors could open. I could see things this way because I know how horrible things were for my mom when my dad died. However, in the end, a new chapter opened up for my mom and many envy her till date. I am not by any means saying it is great for bad things to happen, I am simply saying that painful endings always lead to beautiful beginnings. They always do, so long as the mind of the individual can see that there is something in the future that is far more beautiful that any kind of pain they have experienced. I hoped that soon enough Hadiza would see it, but first, she had to do her surgery.

The surgery was done in the following week and it was very successful. The prognosis of her skin cancer was good anyway, so there was going to be no issues at all. Hadiza who was scared of the idea of a surgery all along was now relieved when it was all over. Then, something that just seemed really unlucky happened. The news of Hadiza's surgery got out and she heard of it soon enough, especially from the whispers in her recovery room. She ended up having to go do the rest of her recovery in a room setup at home and a standby doctor as well as a nurse to ensure that her recovery was very smooth. However, by the time she returned home, she was emotionally tired from everything that had happened. She was in fact almost broken. She hardly spoke to anyone and just did everything that was prescribed for her to fully recover and of course stay alive.

It looked like things would keep going downhill until a skincare brand called her management. They wanted to confirm if the news was true with a report showing evidence, because they had just launched a new product that was specifically produced for people who had experienced skin cancer or anything like it. They wanted Hadiza to join the campaign for Africa. It was a global brand and so far arguably the biggest brand that had called her for a deal since she started modeling.

Her management was thrilled, but wondered how she would feel. It was hard to keep the news after hearing from her assistant, but now, we had to wait for a few days for her to feel even better before telling her. This was the case since we could not afford to have her get worse since her family did not even know she had a surgery. Her management were allowed to always stand the gap for her based on their agreement, so it was no problem. Her issue with telling her family was the fact that her mother would get scared and would not be able to keep the situation to herself. Clearly, this was not a great idea for her own modeling profile.

When we broke the news to her, she was the happiest. "Bring it on!" she said. This was definitely the silver lining she had been looking for in her cloud.

CHAPTER ELEVEN

oming to Lagos was perhaps one of the best decisions I made that year. I now realized that there was a life beyond the "developed=world" bubble within which I lived. The fact was that in spite of how amazing it was to be in Lekki, there was still a lot lacking in the city. The healthcare system designed by the government was horrible. It was the private ones that really served people properly and I mean, the expensive private hospitals that only a few could attend. I was enjoying my time in Lagos because of the culture of the people. They liked to have fun and if you happen to be a newbie among them too, they would love to ensure that you have all that fun too. Lagosians take pride in making foreigners enjoy their stay with them. I loved that and I loved them for that. As Hadiza healed, she had suggested that we all went out to have fun; Amaka, myself and her. I asked her to wait till she was fully healed.

"Time does not wait for us and tomorrow is not promised." She had told me. And as much as I wanted to argue and tell her that she should really be resting, I could not deny the fact that she was correct. I had seen too many people die or lose an important part of their body or its function to cancer. They never got all that time to enjoy life as before again. And sadly, such sicknesses make no announcements before coming. They just come like it is their birth right to do so. I always felt sorry for such people each time but there is really little or nothing that feelings could do in such times, yet all I could do for those people is feel sad and sorry. Thankfully, I am also a volunteer who can help by talking to them, but the truth is that many of them did not even want to talk. Yes, I have talked about a couple of people who wanted to talk and even ended up being friends with me. However, there are some that didn't want to. Yet, whenever I looked into their eyes, I could see a level of pain that their words could not express, at least for that time. Trust me, it was horrible to see that. However, I quickly learnt that I could lend a hand without talking. And I literally lended them my hand because sometimes, all it really took was to hold the hand of the person in pains, as a symbol of the fact that you are there for them and with them.

This was the case with a woman I met in Lagos; Seyi. I could see that she had been through a lot than she could tell me at the time. And all I could just do at the start was hold her hand and let her know that someone was right by her side. It was funny that as much as I had met the affluent in Lagos, there were also others at the other end who were facing serious problems that centered around financial difficult. It did not help that the health system was not amazing too. Seyi was frustrated by all she had been through. I could tell on my first time meeting her. She was not exactly willing to hear anything I had to say and no matter how much I pushed, she already had her walls up and it looked like there was nothing I could do to bring those down. The moment that I asked to hold her hand, she looked at me surprised and there was also a bit of irritation. However, I did not hold her to that. Instead, I insisted on holding her hand no matter what. It looked like she had not exactly experienced any form of expression of love in a while. I could see that. And now, with a child that had cancer, she even seemed more closed off. She did not seem like she was willing to relate with people on a friendship level, even for a start. She acted like a business woman who had so much work to do and could not afford to waste time on things that did not seem so productive; things like making friends. What would that do for her business anyway? And her business in this case was her kids, especially the one with cancer of the sinus. The first day I met her, she was running round the halls of the government hospital to make payments and submit receipts. She had to go to a bank to make her payment. This is a process that has been automated in many developed countries of the world because healthcare is so important. Only one minute of negligence was enough to lose a life, but I was surprised to see how the government system was run here. It was almost like you had to do what you had to irrespective of the condition of the patient. And you could not blame the workers, they don't have that much power, but only work based on policies. It did not also help that many of them did not have active health insurance and even though health insurance does not cover for the treatment of cancers even in many developed countries, it could at least help with basis and give the form of unseen support that Seyi needed at the time. I just really wished the system did a little more better to help people like them, as not everyone in Lagos was as comfortable as Mrs. Cole or Hadiza.

I looked around and could not help, but realize that in the room on the pediatric ward where she was receiving treatment, there were other kids receiving treatment too. It was no private ward and in their corner, I could see the siblings of the child with cancer. They were twins; a boy and a girl. The child with cancer was a girl. I kept looking around because I had now been there in three days, yet, someone was missing in the whole equation and I am not talking about Amaka. Anyway, Amaka had been indisposed herself and needed to rest for a bit before she continued our work, especially since it involved helping the sick. It was just logic that she should not be sick herself. I could wait for her to be back. Being my 5th week, I had now learnt to find my way around relating with Nigerians, but I could not doubt the fact that it would have been more fun with Amaka. I missed her so much.

The person who had been missing in the whole scenario was Seyi's husband. I could not help but wonder where he was in all of this. With all his wife was facing, at least he should be able to come around in the evenings, but no, he was absolutely nowhere to be found. Curiosity made me ask on the third day. I couldn't just hold myself back anymore.

"Where is your husband?" I asked. However, instead of a response, I got her looking at me like I had crossed a line I had no right to cross. I was sorry to have crossed that line, but there wasn't so much I could do now that the words had left my mouth.

"His work must really keep him busy." I said, trying hard to bring the looks and the entire conversation to a polite close. There was quite a long moment of silence between us and I tried hard to say nothing to make things awkward and trust me; that was really hard. Something in me wanted to say something; I wanted to say anything, but instead of that, I decided that I would take a bathroom break. So, off I went to the bathroom, to do absolutely nothing. Then I decided that staring at the mirror was far better than doing literally nothing. So, I stared at the mirror and thought of those days in high school when I would take a bathroom break to avoid an awkward conversation. Well, after five minutes had passed, I went right back to that ward in the oncology unit and sat there. By now, Seyi was standing and I could her breath loudly. It seemed she had been panting, but beyond that, there was something else. Then she turned to look at me and I could see what it was. She had been crying.

"Is anything wrong with Precious?" I quickly flung up from my seat, making a move to go call someone, if something was really wrong with the child.

"No, nothing is wrong with her." She said softly. It was my first time hearing her speak so softly, but it sounded very much like her nature.

"You asked about her father. Well, he left. He left us alone yet again when Precious was diagnosed with cancer. The painful part is that this is not his first time of doing so. The first time, he promised not do so ever again, but look where we are. We are all by ourselves again. The twins are four years old and he left without paying the bills when they were born. The hospital had to call my sister who lives in another city to come pay and get us. My sister had to drive all the way down from her city to come help. One month later, Wale showed up begging and saying he was too scared after the kids were born and that was why he ran away." She let out a loud cry and I quickly tried to calm her down and told those around that there was nothing to worry about, by the signals I made with my hand.

"Why would he say that? Didn't you do a scan before the kids came?"

"Of course he knew we were going to have twins. He just said that on carrying them, he felt like it was too much for him to handle and he was not sure he was the best for them, so he left to God knows where. Up to now, I don't know where he stayed for a whole month following their birth and each time I tried to ask him about where he stayed, he just kept saying that he was really sorry and that there was so much that he could not explain, but I should bear with him and forgive him. It was a horrible place to be because this was a man I love and I did not want to raise the kids alone, so I had to let it go. After all, he said he would change."

"And did he change?"

"Wale, who already had a drinking problem, came home to me drunk almost every night till the twins were about seven months old. He would say he was scared and I just had to encourage him to be a better father, because he did not know how. He said I just had to keep trying and never give up on him. I was nursing twins with the help of my younger sister, who came around when she was not so busy in school. However, with the kind of husband he was being, it felt like I was nursing another child. Asides getting food ready for his return, I always had to counsel him every night in the hopes that he was really clueless and he was really going to change. I did not know that my calculations had been wrong and I had only been fooling myself with him all along. I just wish I knew better."

"If you knew better, you would have done better. Those are the words I say to myself when I remember the mistakes I made in the past. Then I suppose he didn't change."\

"He didn't. The only time he stopped for a while was when he was not making a lot of money from his mechanic shop. And that was the only reason he stopped. It was like that for two months and then, he continued again. But look where we are now, he said he would change, but once Precious was diagnosed, he disappeared into the thin air again."

The worst part about everything was the fact that she couldn't call her family as they had already asked her never to take back such an irresponsible man that brought nothing to the table, but she had gone back to him and frankly, it takes a lot of strength to get rid of someone you are very used to. So, I totally got it. I just felt sorry for her and the kids. Shed reiterated how she did not her kids to grow up without a father figure, so she had put in all her energy to seeing him stay and perhaps, making him change, but she had failed at that. So she wished she hadn't tried from the start. She wished she had let go and not wasted an extra four years on a Leopard that would never change its skin.

"It is not your fault." I said to her. "The most important thing about life is not that we never make mistakes, but that we are able to realize our mistakes and make amends, so we can move on the right way and never repeat the same pattern again. The fact that he left the first time and yet again, that's all on him and not you. You are a dedicated woman who has stayed strong for her family. You have been the parent your kids could rely on and that is a lot. Seyi, you should be proud of yourself." I could that she was in her late twenties and had started having kids in her early twenties.

"There is still a whole lot ahead of you. Your past may look like it has already taken a huge chunk out of your life, but trust me, there is a better future waiting for you and you merely need to tap into that future. You need to move forward knowing that you did all you could for your past to be better and the fact that it did not turn out great is not your fault in any way. The fact that you waited to see him change is all the closure you need, but you can probably tell that it was not worth your time."

"What if he comes back begging?" she asked.

"What if he leaves again?" I asked.

"There is so much to your life. There is so much more you could do for yourself and the last thing you need is to have a man that draws you back. An amazing woman like you who is very dedicated needs a strong man to stay by your side and support you in your quest to achieve your dreams, not some man that pulls you back."

"Dreams?"

"Yes, dreams."

"With my kids?"

"Of course."

"Look, you can argue that I have never been married. However, I am not talking about something I have not seen before or trying to build a castle in the air. I have seen such a loving relationship between my parents and I know for sure that men support their women. Thinking that no man would support your dreams or help you grow even outside the home is what would fetch you bad men that won't support you. Imagine having a husband that shares in the responsibility of caring for the kids and doesn't just leave you to do all the work by yourself."

"That would be really good." She said.

"But can I find such a man with three kids."

"I won't lie to you and this may break your heart. Honestly, I don't know if you would. That is why moving on to get a man isn't such an excellent idea. While having a great man is amazing; that cannot be your goal or you may get yourself heartbroken if you don't. However, it is a possibility. It is a possibility which is a better reality than what you currently have. Trust me, it is far better than what you have experienced and I am sure you know that too."

"I just want support. Taking care of my kids and now, Precious' cancer cannot be such an easy task. It is not easy in anyway, especially emotionally and financially. I am still trying to raise more money for her surgery. If I wasn't alone, it would have been better. The burden would be for two people and not just me."

She had contacted our support group because of the support she needed. I could see the posters of the branch in Lagos all over the oncology unit of the hospital and I was really glad that she reached out and they sent me down to help. At least, our own little system was working and I was thankful for that. Life could be a lot better with support for real. I liked the way Seyi had eased into our conversation. Problems become less burdensome when they are shared. I was happy that I could help, but I kept emphasizing that her runaway husband was no support but an extra stressor for her. I really hoped she would work with that truth, because men like that always came back. I know a little about such situations thanks to the neighborhood in which I grew up, where I had seen a couple of such examples. I wished something new could quickly happen to her to confirm that sh did not need to care about a man that left when she needed him the most. I really wished so.

She resorted to raising funds and I had to give her all the support I knew how to. Her family had told her that they had no money to give her and from the little she had told me about them, it seemed true that they did not have money to give her. However, their decision was influenced by her sister who had told them how she had warned her never to go back to her husband, Wale. It took a lot to get to a place where she could say she'll just go raise funds.

"How do you plan to do that?" I asked.

"I would go to the streets and talk from person to person. I would explain my situation to them and just maybe, I would go from one office to another and explain the situation of my child to them."

"And they would be willing to help you?" I asked, looking from her to Amaka, who was now in great shape and had now resumed. "And you would be able to raise the amount you need?" I asked without waiting for the reply to my initial question.

Now I could see the look on Seyi's face. The worth of the money was over one million in Nigeria currency, naira. Personally, I did not think begging from one person to another would do the trick with getting all that money.

"Amaka, do things work like that here?" I asked.

It was our fourth day with Seyi and the next day, Friday, was going to be our last official day with her. However, we could also come on the weekend, even though it was optional to do so.

"I don't think doing that would work. People are more careful with giving out money these days. You could try, but I don't think raising money that way is a great idea." Said Amaka.

"In that case, I am thinking we could use social media to advantage." I said.

"Twitter is an effective app for that. Nigerians love twitter and I have seen people use it to raise funds over and over. To be honest, I think it's our best bet." Amaka added.

And on that note, we knew that we had to open a twitter account for Seyi and make sure all that money gets raised in the few days we had before the time the surgery was scheduled for. It seemed crazy, but we planned to try.

"But what was your plan to get the money before now?"

"I just felt like God would make a way." Said Seyi.

This made Amaka turn her head away. She had talked about how a major issue she had with Nigerians was the fact that they were always placing responsibilities on God without making any effort whatsoever about doing their part. She had complained bitterly about that behavior to me, but she knew it was not a good time to talk to Seyi about the whole concept and why she thought it was wrong to think like that. There was a long pause and I decided to break the ice by asking questions about the twins, their level of education and everything else about them. Honestly, I was just trying to cover up the way things were left without being awkward in anyway.

That evening, Amaka and I got on twitter and did our thing. We also asked our friends to keep retweeting our tweets. While hers retweeted from Nigeria and some from Canada, my own friends retweeted from the United States. Honestly, the story was such a touching one and in no time, we started to receive donations.

"Perhaps, Seyi's thoughts about how God would make a way at such a critical time is what has actually worked in this moment." I said jokingly, but since we were now alone, it looked like my dear friend was now ready to dissect the issue.

"She did not even say she prayed or she thought, she only said that she felt God would somehow make a way. That makes absolutely no sense. And even if God is going to make a way, you have to take action. And this is the issue I have with religious folks in this country. You can't wake up and decide not to get a job, but say God would make a way or God would bless you. Even if God wants to bless you, of course, he blesses the works of your hands and just makes you prosper. And that is exactly what you call a blessing. However, people just need to learn to take action. Her statement showed that she was not expecting to do anything new, but she expected God to provide the way a magician brings his shiny cap out of the thin air. I really doubt that things work that way. At least, from the little I have seen, God just blesses the works of your hand. If we did not come on twitter and do massive retweeting, we would have nothing pouring in. Sometimes, what God even gives us is strategies to get the blessings."

"…and tweeting the way we have been tweeting to get this money is definitely a strategy."

"Of course, it is." My friend laughed.

Gradually, the money started pouring in. It came in all forms of foreign currency. We decided not to exactly give Seyi much details until we got half of what was needed. Funnily, the turn out was massive and within 24 hours, we got half of the money we needed for the surgery. It was amazing because the next week, we had to move to the next patient as our time with Seyi would be over. We told her about the turn out and she jumped for joy. She was overwhelmed. In the next eight hours, we got all the money Precious needed for her surgery and it was a different level of fulfilment for me. I was happy to just see that I was able to put a smile on Seyi's face and just make her daughter's life better in the little way that I could.

Even when we announced that we had gotten all we needed, people were still asking to donate for the upkeep of the child following the surgery, especially if we would still need chemo. The kids from my high school that had seen my tweet and donated were numerous. It was amazing to see that they had matured to an extent. Who ever thought? Well, who thought the unserious me would be in Africa at this time of my life, helping a kid with cancer who had no money for surgery. I was definitely not the type my friends thought would do that in high school, but I guess people could really change in a very short while. Well, about this particular change, I was super proud of myself. However, that is really a story for another day. My focus for the time being was still to have Precious do her surgery.

And she did it. She was scared at first, and Amaka and I had to work on her confidence a bit. We designed cards all around her bed and her corner on the ward just to remind her that she was truly loved. We also wrote quotes that she could chant in the morning, during the day and at night before she slept. The theme of everything was "warrior". We just wanted to remind her that she was a warrior and she could fight anything and win, including the cancer. We wanted to remind her that we were there to support her throughout the time and the doctors just wanted her to feel better. She had grown fond of me and Amaka too, when she joined us. She had begun to see us as "big sister" figures, so she really trusted in what we told her and we also tried our best to keep living up to what would thought would be her expectations of us, so we would not break her trust in any way. Now, I could understand why many people supposedly live for their kids. Many people even think of committing suicide, but decide not to do it again, just because of their kids. When it came to kids, I could now see that it was the kind of responsibility that makes you want to be better, so you can give them better too.

"The surgery is only another chance for you to beat the cancer. Don't be scared of it, because it is the very solution you need. Can you imagine a world with no solutions to diseases?"

She shook her head.

"Exactly kiddo. You now have that solution and you should not be scared of it because once the surgery is over, you would feel a lot better."

A cancer was luckily in its early stage, so a surgery to fish out the bad cells in nasal sinus would make her better and get her back in good shape. By the day of the surgery, our girl felt all charged up and ready to become good once again. I was happy to see her this way and we all waited patiently for her to be wheeled into the recovery room. By the time she got better and we tweeted about it, there were gifts from all over the place for her. It was the beginning of my last week in Nigeria and honestly, I was not supposed to be with Precious anymore, but because of the good work and all the fund raising we had started, our coordinators had asked us to carry on with the patient and we were more than glad to do so. In fact, Precious and her mother, Seyi, were happy at the news. This is why we were able to witness her surgery and then, her recovery. Honestly, I would have regretted it if I did not get a chance to be there for those times.

The show of love was unreal and it was also a proof that everywhere in the world, there were good humans who were just willing to help others. It was those people from social media who were in Lagos that trooped in to celebrate her recovery.

The best part of everything for me was when Seyi confessed to us that our actions had given her hope. The words she said brought so much joy to my heart that I cannot deny. I am glad that our time with her ended with those amazing words.

In her words, "I was at a time in my life when I had lost hope about life and all I wanted to do was return to what I was familiar with; my estranged husband, pain and hurt. I thought life would be easier if I stayed with what I knew. However, you guys came and I realized that new situations could be far better than what I have always known. You came into my life and I believe God used you to give me hope about life and the health of my child. Look at us, you brought so much laughter into our midst and I am just glad that I was able to meet you guys." She had said.

Moments like those, proved that we were truly making real impact and it brought so much joy to my heart to see that. I never for once regretted my journey to Nigeria because of the reports of this kind of impact and especially seeing that we were part of the process to get a child like Precious back to her usual life.

From Mrs. Cole to Hadiza to every other patient I met in Lagos and of course, Precious; I could see that the outcome of every process is different for each purpose and success in each case was to be measured very differently. I was glad about each success in its own rights.

CHAPTER TWELVE

A genius with lung cancer. That is a very rare and awkward mix, isn't it? The last thing that comes to mind when you hear of a genius is the fact that they could have their vices. Or maybe everyone has their vices and that is okay. Perhaps, some just have vices that are morally acceptable while others don't. That is probably pretty much the truth. So, being a genius, does it really stop a smoker from smoking? Or anyone from their addictions; any addiction at all? Maybe the addiction fuels the love of this genius for his expertise that he is being recognized for and in cases like this, it is pretty hard to take a person away from the source of their own inspiration, as Mr. Louis loved to call it. And oh, he's Nigerian and I met him in Nigeria. We had ended up spending an extra week in Nigeria because everyone was enjoying it. I saw the news sometimes about the unbecoming things that the government was doing, but we had been shielded by location and protection, so it was no problem for us. Hence, we stayed a week more and once again, Amaka and I were seeing an interesting patient. Once again, I wondered if others were getting to see distinct scenarios too. Sometimes, we picked up cases to discuss as case studies and how we could help. During such discussions, the name of the patient was not usually mentioned for the purpose of privacy. The person speaking just brings up the condition of a patient they had seen, and then, they tell us what they did to help while we thought out other ways through which the help they had rendered to the person would have been better. I really enjoyed these sections, as we had never done this back at home and I could only hope that Mr. Andrew was taking notes. About him, he had spoken to my mother on a few more nights when we were partying and I could not just hear my phone ring. However, I doubted that would lead anywhere as their conversations always seemed a little drab compared to what that of two true new lovers would sound like. Frankly, I think Lagos had distracted him a bit too and I liked that. The part of me that thinks very far cannot just imagine being my stepfather. I think that would be a horrible idea. He would probably do better for someone else, but certainly not me. Or maybe I did not just want any stepfather at all. We have lived without father all this while, we definitely do not need any extra trouble. You know humans and what it takes to warm up to them; especially the fact that we would now be family.

I think the concept of family is a really deep one. The fact that even if you don't talk in months, you should be willing to come through when I need you is deep. The fact that you can dislike someone in the moment, but you can't stop loving them because you are related by blood, you ae family—that's pretty deep. You don't just give such privileges to anyone and everyone or you would end up having yourself surrounded by intruders, yet being obligated to them. Well, in the end, the ball is majorly in my mother's court; whether she made him family or not. Or maybe I was indeed thinking too far. Mr. Andrew probably only wanted a good time and some companionship. However, my mother is a different kind of woman. I doubt that any man would come so close and not end up falling in love with her. And you know; love is love, there is no antidote for it. Even if things get horrible, you have to love your way through the situation until perhaps, the love fizzles out by itself. Love determines when it comes and when it leaves; and there is absolutely nothing you can do about that. So, what happens when he falls in love and thinks he wants to spend the rest of his life with her? I am sure my siblings will cringe on hearing stuff like because damn! What is that? I don't want to think much about it.

Well, I started thinking this deep about family and the possibility of Mr. Andrew joining mine from the time I started seeing my patient because of the man's situation. Or maybe relating with geniuses just made you think a bit deeper about everything in this world. That is probably why I found myself doing the whole genius analysis thing earlier on. Family is indeed an important aspect of life as well as an important aspect of socialization. The presence or the lack of family could make a huge difference in a person's life. It could influence how much they do with their lives and career. Even more, it may influence their motivations and their definitions of what they want out of life and when this is the case (in this case, a bad scenario where there is a lack of family), you can't exactly blame the individual, especially if you have not walked in their shoes. The patient Amaka and I had been assigned to, had been angry at life for too long, yet he did not stop doing well at his craft.

From what we read of him, we realized that he hardly ever talked to anyone, but instead, he focused on his craft—writing, and was considered a genius at that owing to the several awards he had received, as well as those he had been nominated for. However, from what I could see on meeting him, I did not think that he actually cared that much about his achievements. He just wanted to do more from what I could see.

I wondered if this was how every man who lost their family in a fire acted, or if it was just how this particular guy liked to act. Mr. Louis, whose father happened to be a British writer (who is now late) and his mother, a Nigerian, decided to settle in Nigeria as he loved the people and the nation as a whole. Apparently, while this happened, he wasn't the only one settling, his father's writing skills had settled with him too. However, he progressed in his law career and also established a couple of businesses which he managed. He did not only build businesses, he also got married to the love of his life, Helen, and built a family with her too. They were blessed with a set of twins and they were raising them happily until the day he came home to the ugly incident. Not just his house, but his entire family was on fire and there was almost nothing he could do about that. The fire service did not come to the scene as early as they should have. This is because it was a mansion and the fire had actually started from their living quarters, with his wife and his kids sleeping in it. By the time the fumes were noticed and the fire service was on their way, the entire family had actually burnt to ashes. By the time he got to the scene after he got a call, he tried to run into the fire but onlookers held him back and made sure he did not run into the fire. They were now gone and there was almost nothing he could do about that. They put out the fire, but the house became useless to him without the presence of his family. He was quite a popular man, so it was not surprising that his story spread quickly. It is well-known Nigerian story, as he was a well-known business man. After the fire, he walked out of the house and never returned again. As Mrs. Cole had found time to narrate the story to us; she said that the house remains desolate up to today.

In her words, "Everyone just passes by the house and sighs. Those who knew when the house was great can only bow their heads in despair each time they remember the story. His wife was a member of a couple of women societal groups and she was indeed loved by many. It was a very sad thing to see her pass like that. Till today, we wonder what the cause of the fire was. The entire portion of that building burnt down and the staff had left for the day, as they liked to have evenings as time for only family. Mr. Louis was not interested in any police investigation about what might have happened or anything that involved the house at all. However, there was a rumor that the fire came from the kitchen, but I don't think he cared one bit. I don't think he has said anything about the incident or talked to anyone about it till today. From his book, we could only see that he had a philosophy that when a person dies, there is no amount of searching you could ever do to bring that person back. No amount of investigation could ever be done to make a dead person come back to life, as he had written in one of his numerous books."

Indeed, Mr. Louis' writing capabilities had come to life after he lost his family. It was as though that was what kept him sane. What I did not understand was why he decided to live in a house full of cracks in the wall. The windows were also cracked. It was a very old house. Luckily, his lawyer could trace him to this new house he had moved to. He told his lawyer to sell everything he had and give half of the proceeds to charity, except of course the house where his family had died. He did not want to have anything to do with that house. The cracked house where he lived was a very small bungalow he had bought to re-construct, and then, use for a new business. He had asked his lawyer to also shut up the process of starting up that business. And despite the fact that he had the entire bungalow to himself, he only used one of the rooms where he had a bed, a table, a chair and then, two extra chairs for whoever had to come looking for him. He lived on canned food and even though he had a lot of money from the sales of everything he had, there were absolutely no signs that he was spending all that money on anything in particular. In my opinion, he was living miserably and I hoped that there was something I could do to help him, but he was not even the type to open up. He didn't seem he was ready to socialize even though he had lost his family about five years ago. The only good thing that had come out from his misfortune was his gift that was forced to manifest and even at that, it was his lawyer (who was about the only person he talked to), that forced him to publish the book. He wrote from his wooden table and chair in his cracked house day and night and I could see that if he had his way, the books he wrote with his pen would be buried in dust somewhere in that room. His lawyer forced the reluctant Louis to publish book after book and it landed him recognition from all over the world. I did not care about who was nominated for Nobel Prizes, if not, I would have noticed him and his achievements while I was in the states. Now, when I looked at him, there was something I could see for sure. He was punishing himself for the death of his wife and his kids and if he did not think he had done enough, he won't stop. I felt like if he kept thinking this way, he would punish himself for life because nothing he did would be ever enough to quench how he felt—guilty.

I had arrived at this line of thinking together with Amaka. "This man is a highly principled man and they are usually very stubborn."

"I agree. Although he feels like he cannot bring them back, at least, he can make amends for not being there for them. He obviously wishes he would have died with them." She said.

I couldn't agree less. If he did not think that he should have died with them, he wouldn't pick up the horrible smoking habits he had picked up. It looked like he did not go a day without smoking. We were told that it helped him write. He was now being treated in one of the rooms in that bungalow and it was the help that helped us with some information about how he had been acting.

"Even now, he still asks for a stick in spite of his diagnosis. He doesn't seem to care much. He still scribbles things from time to time, but it is obvious that smoking has been his habit for a long time. Before his lawyer employed me, he wanted to know if I was a smoker. He wouldn't have employed me if I was. He said I have to make sure he doesn't get a stick and I have even heard them get into arguments sometimes because he had been smoking. That seems to help with the writing, as he had complained that being sober makes him rather uninspired, but the instruction I have is never to do anything that encourages him to indulge in smoking."

To think that something that could kill him was the same thing that brought the genius in him to life was just crazy. How was that even possible? But I realized that this happened a lot of the time to many people. I just feel this way now because this is someone that is supposed to be a genius who had apparently always just done his work under the influence.

"I was employed just before his diagnosis because his health was deteriorating and the coughing would not just subside. He was also becoming increasingly weak and could not do a lot of things around the house, so he definitely needed help. Hence, his lawyer employed me.

When he got diagnosed, he did not seem to be moved one bit. He did not seem bothered about the fact that his lungs were in shambles and he was almost at the final stage of the cancer of the lungs. I don't think he had gotten over his family one bit. He hasn't moved on. He still wants to go back to how things used to be and I don't think he minds dying if he can't get that. Of course, he could never get that again."

The man had been depressed for a long time and had written in spite of his depression. That was probably a great distraction for him. The fact that he had to appear a couple of times to receive awards was another distraction. Even though he appeared unkempt and looking very awkward and rough, at least he showed up and was able to see other humans. Most of the time, he stayed indoors and just ordered for canned foods to eat. He ate a little, but he obviously smoked a lot. We were able to learn many things from what the help had observed as well as the conversations he had heard Louis have with his lawyer. Now that he had insisted that he be treated in a room setup with all the facilities for his care, in his bungalow and healthcare professionals resuming round the clock to treat him. However, it was advised that he had people who were just lively around him for a while because from what they could see; his behavioral pattern and the fact that he insisted on being treated at home, it was very possible that he was planning a suicide. He had the tendencies and his lung cancer could be the perfect excuse he had been looking for to end things by himself. Euthanasia is not legal in Nigeria, so he could not ask them to pull the plug on him, but he may really also not want to wait to get treatment or even see how he responds to treatment and his prognosis. He had always wanted to die and had probably found the perfect excuse. This was why Amaka and I were with him at this time. We were not with him to talk to him or anything, as it was very obvious that he would not respond. So, we went there and sat by him. Sometimes, we took turns to go to the help and ask questions. This was only out of our curiosity.

It was the same curiosity that made us ask about him from Mrs. Cole. We had done this without letting her know that we had any contact with him. We just went to her as two curious girls, just looking to learn from whatever she had to say about the man; and that we did. We learnt his sad story and as the days went by, it became increasingly difficult to keep quiet while we were by his side. We were told he loved his clients, but there were many things my friend and I wanted to ask him. We wanted to engage him in conversations as we felt like that may really encourage him to want to live. The truth is, we all need something to live for. As for him, he seemed to have even peaked his writing career which he just started a few years back. He was fulfilled and should probably be living for family, as it was obvious that this was how he felt. However, there was no family to live for. This was really his plight.

"Shortness of breath and non-stop coughing, severe fatigue, nausea and loss of appetite, build-up of fluid around the lungs." The doctor said, as he announced that Louis' was indeed at the end stage of lung cancer and that he could say his goodbyes anytime soon or he won't. As for us, we were still in Nigeria because we had to spend yet another one week due to logistics, but I really did not care much. It was fine. I was young and of course, still enjoying my time in the city of Lagos. Louis had been only receiving palliative care all along and it had now been announced that he had only little time left.

Honestly, it wasn't that surprising because as always, when it came to the final stage of most cancers as I know, palliative care is the option until the patient packs up. As for palliative care, it involves caring for a person that you know would die soon. It involves just taking care of them and allowing them feel better while they are still alive while not trying to cure them or take them through any stressful means of treatment. It was really sad to know that a person was being cared for that way. It was basically the medical field saying, "This can't be cured, so we would just what we can do to make you feel better till you die." I think that is really bad, but it is what it is. Anyway, we had been doing guess work all along and the doctor confirmed that our guess was somewhat accurate by telling us that in times like this especially, the cancer patient needed all those who were close to them to rally round them and give them all the support they needed.

In this case, Louis' family was gone. He was not one to have exactly kept friends close. He was more of loner, but had a few close colleagues from his law practice. However, he had chased them away from coming around in the past. He had said that they were bad people and he wanted nothing with them. That hurt them a lot and vowed never to come around to see him, which was exactly what he wanted. He had denied people access to his life up to that point and that is why volunteers were needed in this case. You may be wondering if our superiors never gave us any information about his case. Well, they didn't. They just told us that we may not have to do more than just being present with him. We didn't need to encourage him or anything. And that was what we found. It was just a bit awkward sitting by him and smiling all day. They say that is what family would probably do, but I highly doubted that. If I was his daughter, I'd probably sit with him with a stack of fashion magazines and read them one after the other, since I just needed sit with him like a statue there. I was there with my friend, but it was very improper for us to talk and gist in such a setting, except it was with the patient. And our patient did not seem like he had time on his hands for gist. He spent all day in his head and just looked at us with what I believe is disdain, from time to time. It was horrible to realize that he was looking at us through his glasses in that manner. We were good people who were dedicating our time through volunteering to be with him. We didn't deserve to be looked on like that for any reason and by anyone at all; no matter how high and mighty they thought themselves to be.

He still wore his glasses, the type those scholars usually wore, so you can imagine a scholar shifting down his glasses to his nose level just to turn and look at you with disdain. That was exactly what he kept doing to us. He did it from to time in this particular week when it was said that he could die anytime soon. He looked at us like we didn't know what we were doing, then he would go back to trying to read the daily times again, only for him to wince in pain and have his nurse come around to check up on him. At some point, the way he looked at us quickly as if he did not want us to notice, before turning back to his newspaper made me want to laugh. It was so funny, especially with all that curly white hair he had on his face, I figured that this is because of his British descent. It was just so funny, he really looked like some English professor. He had not been trimming his hair and he let his help trim it for him only once since the guy started working with him. I think he was just a stubborn person, but all his hairs were really out of place. And as expected, he did not care. I guess it was part of his costume. What a man!

After the doctor had left earlier that morning, his lawyer came later in the day and we told him what the doctor had said. He did not seem surprised by what we told him at all.

"Did you just really get to know all these?" He asked us.

"Yes!" We replied simultaneously and abruptly. Apparently, his dear lawyer had assumed that we had an intensive conversation previously about the state of things with Mr. Louis, which we didn't. It looked like our dear lawyer was also aging fast, but that is just for laughs.

"I am sorry that I haven't filled you up on all these till now. In all honesty, I thought I had and now feel terrible to know that I didn't fill you in all along. What a shame!" He said.

"Of course." Amaka muttered under her breath. I gave her a knowing look. It had been frustrating all along especially to her, that they had treated the information about Mr. Louis like knowing about his condition, as we rightfully should, would only bring us into a secret cult. If you ask me, that was very annoying. It was literally our right for us to know, but we thought he was such a high profile patient that they couldn't trust us with all that information. This is why we had to go as far as trying to know what Mrs. Cole knew about him. Looking back on that, it was a bit of a desperate move and our only saving grace was the fact that we had kept the fact that we were now with him private. Instead, we made it look like we came to see Mrs. Cole and I, being a foreigner, had heard one or two things and just needed to hear what she knew about the story. You could trust that she was excited to tell us. I think the fact that a foreigner was interested in hearing such a story thrilled her even more; well, I think.

"His cancer is at stage 4B. It has spread not only to areas around his lungs, but also to another areas in his body—inclusive of organs and bones. He cannot go under radiation because he might not even be able to stand the effect of it or survive through the process of getting treated through it. He was too weak; his entire body system was just too weak to handle all that. He has been taking performance tests from time to time, to help us know how the cancer was progressing. The stage of his cancer is why he had to be at home all this while. In such cases, it was best to be close to what you knew as home and have those who you could family stay around you at such a time, and that is why you guys are here. That is why we needed you as volunteers to just stay by him, not encouraging him, but just letting him know that he is not alone."

"…but he scoffs at us every time. And he doesn't allow the help to help him in any way. He just seems to be fine by himself. He does not want to eat too. He acts like he doesn't need anyone." Amaka complained bitterly.

"We both know that everyone needs someone, especially this amazing man who is in this particular state. He has been acting this way since he lost his family. It would definitely be hard for him to change at this point, but trust me, a dying man wants to be surrounded by people he thinks care about him. His colleagues from his law practice, he always felt like they never really cared; hence, he doesn't want them around him. He never saw them as friends. However, as for you guys, he talks to me a few times and tells me he has done everything he knew how to just to let you go, but you just would not go. He actually thinks you care about him and now, he definitely wants you to stay with him."

This brought smiles to our faces; the help inclusive. I guess for Mr. Louis, he was just stubborn, as a Leopard would definitely not change its spots very easily. It was not like he was a wicked or heartless person. As we continued talking, we heard a voice from his room, so we went in to see. It was him talking.

"If you guys are going to have a meeting or anything, you know you can't leave me out, right?" He said as we walked right back in.

"Family don't do that. You can't just leave me out of your conversations. That's very unfair." He said. "Barrister Siji, I did not think you in particular, would do that to me."

The barrister was about to start explaining when Mr. Louis burst into laughter. Turns out he was only joking about the whole thing after all.

It was amazing to see that he finally saw us as family. It was amazing to hear from the barrister that he had thought about us this way all along. I was really fulfilled to know that all our days here had not been wasted all along. He actually appreciated it.

"When you guys were gone, Jane came around. She said the kids missed me. Well, I told her I missed them too, but really, Jane should not come here. She has no business here." I said.

With the way he was talking, it was not hard to figure out that the Jane he was talking about was his late wife.

"I miss her." He said. "She said I could come join her. She said I would stop feeling the pain I feel if I come join her. I think she was correct. It won't be bad to see the kids too." I said.

It was obvious that he was about to go. We looked at ourselves and bowed our heads to the ground. We knew it was almost time to say goodbye to an icon.

"Is there anything you would like to tell me?" asked the Barrister.

When we saw that he was about to talk, we started to leave, so we could let him have some privacy with his lawyer.

"No, it's fine. You can stay." Louis said.

He winced. He was in pain. "Remember the last amendment I made to my will, let's keep things that way." He said. And then, he passed.

We got money, he gave myself, Amaka and the help lots of money. As for the house he never went back to, he asked his lawyer to give it to our support group, along with enough money to renovate it and some extra donations. The remaining of his money was to be given to charity; different groups across Nigeria. The impact of all that money was felt, as I later heard. Indeed, he exited like an icon.

CHAPTER THIRTEEN

We went to Cape Verde and we did it without much thinking. I was not sure if it was the fact that we were just young and wild, the fact that we were drunk the night that we had decided that we would go there or just the fact that Mr. Louis had left a lot of money in naira (well, according to Amaka) for us. I never even converted the money to see what its equivalent would be in US dollars; I just started with the spending and booking of tickets. We did not need visas to go there, so we did not have to do much thinking to go there. My mother and Mr. Andrews had been talking back and forth to monitor me and he had been doing well to tell her my location at every time. However, when it was time for me to go to Cape Verde, I did well to remind him that my mother would not grant him a date if I did not influence it in any way.

I had to help him in some way and he couldn't agree less; my mother was quite a "babe" if you know what I mean. On my part, I could not get my mother bothered about the fact that I was going to an Island in Africa. In order to keep her from bothering, I had to strike a deal with him to tell her I was still working in Nigeria. After all, although the other volunteers were returning to the states soon, he was staying back, so why not tell her that I was in Nigeria, safe with him. I was one of the best volunteers after all. She did not even know that many other volunteers were coming along in the first place, thanks to how he had presented the case to her from the start, just to get a date. I guess this is part of the highs of having a mother that was pretty, even while she was aging. Or maybe, just maybe Mr. Andrews was just more interested in older women—well, maybe. Maybe he was one of those men that just believed that the older the berry, the sweeter the wine. Well, good for him. The long and short of it was that I was on the winning end and that was all I really cared about. He could worry about the other details, for all I cared. Honestly, I wished him good luck. In my opinion, men go through a lot to get the "woman of their dreams" or maybe it's just the "woman they want". Anyway, I have learnt to care less as the times I cared hard for a few friends, they even tried harder at getting the woman they wanted without even caring about how detrimental it might have been to their image. I don't think a man cares much about his image when he is trying to get a particular woman. Maybe that's a bit pathetic that it is a game their gender actually enjoys. However, who am I to talk about that? My gender has little or no games to play. Well, I am not talking about the relationship aspect. There, you could fiddle with a man that wants you as a game to amuse yourself. However, in life generally, video games are not supposed to be for women. Football and other sporting activities for women are not seen as very feminine. In the end, in our minds, thanks to the stereotypes built over the years, it is always a matter of a woman trying hard at a man's game, to show that they can also do well at it. However, we play each other and get mocked when we act feminine during these games because it is a taboo to act in feminine ways like scream while playing football. It all buoys down to the fact that in the end, they are not feminine games.

So, what games do females even have? We don't have games. We have fashion and lifestyle. We have the concept of looking colorful and beautiful. This is why I don't understand women that don't care about these things because self-care is the ultimate game for us and how well you do at it influences many things in your life as a woman. How good you look and how groomed you are will definitely go a long way in determining how well men and even women would want to treat you. At least, once in every woman's life, she would have met that other woman she admired so much and wanted to be her friend so badly. Or maybe there are some that have literally been that kind of woman who is desired by both sexes all their lives. There are definitely women like that and I can say this from what I saw and experienced firsthand in high school, or maybe I can't because I can't say if those girls that were so glamorous back then in high school are still the most glamorous girls on their college campuses in the moment. Anyway, everyone has their lives to live and should determine what phase it should be for them at every point in their lives. Who says girls can only be glamorous? What I have explained is that it is one of our own major games—a way to cool off. You know, just looking beautiful, like the star of the evening. This is definitely a way to relax.

All of this is what led Amaka and I on a shopping spree in Lekki, Nigeria, right before our travels. It was only normal for us to shop for clothes, shoes and bags. We had enough to spend and we were so young. Mr. Andrew of course knew of our sudden fortune and we had done our bit by throwing a party for the whole group. They were grateful for this and we were more than happy to be able to provide a good time for the small family we had in Nigeria.

In view of our travels, self-care was also very important to us. We did not joke with our facials, manicure and pedicure appointments. We really wanted to feel good and that was self-care did. It give you a level of beauty which is not only seen, but also felt. It was the kind of beauty that cae with being a confident woman. And when you have that kind of beauty combined with the physical attributes that go with it, you would then be referred to as an elegant woman and that was exactly what we were shooting for, even though we had not defined it at the time. We were just so engrossed in looking our best. We were always so engrossed in our discussions about our beauty and travel plans that we did not pay much attention to other people that were trying to be friends with us. Honestly, we were not trying to be snobbish in any way. We were sincerely making plans about things that concerned and it got other volunteers (before they left) talking about the fact that we had grown proud, but really, we were just the same two fun-loving and carefree beautiful ladies that we had been all along. For once, I understood from the other side of the cliff. I understood that those girls and ladies that I once used to see as full of themselves were probably just busy doing their thing and not caring much about any other person, because they were so busy with themselves. And is that not how it ought to be? Are we not supposed to be engrossed with our own lives that we have little or no time to talk about what the next person is doing or not doing; right or wrong? Well, I came to the conclusion that at different points in our lives, we get the understanding of different things and the fact that we did not understand a certain concept at a time does not mean we should belittle it or just talk bad about those who understand it or are already functioning on a particular level because of their understanding of some things. It could equally also be their way of seeing life. Guess what? It is okay and I feel like if people really understood this, life would be indeed very much better. When I say life would get better, I say so because I mean that the quality of people would be much better.

Oh! And I really need to mention the part when the other volunteers were going to the airport, but Amaka's mum came to pick me because I was staying over at theirs till it was time for our own travels. Amaka lived with her mum alone. She was an only child and her father had passed. I could not help, but imagine how you could really have someone with similar experiences, a similar understanding about life and a personality that just suited yours somewhere half way across the world. I guess this is why it is so important to travel with every chance we get. Well, now you can see why it is that important and if the seamless friendship between Amaka and I has not inspired you so far, I wonder what could really inspire you. Haha! I guess there would be something else out there that would inspire you to travel and I wish you the very best in your findings, my dear reader.

Amaka's mother was amazing. She was totally the kind of mother that had refused to grow old and she also had amazing friends. They were all so cool or maybe it was just the glow that was rumored to be popular among women that were over the age of fifty and had either lost their husband or were just divorced. They always glowed different and it was usually very beautiful to see. She was very open to hear all our escapades so far and she didn't judge our thoughts like an elderly woman at all. She was really open-minded and I could see so many similarities between my mother and her. It explained why Amaka and I were so compatible. I am not saying we did not have our quarrels and challenges as every friendship had that. However, the good outweighed the bad to an outrageously large extent such that the bad had little influence over our relationship. I could not be grateful enough for the gift of her and I could see that she felt the same. It had only been a little above six weeks since we met and I could say that she was one of the best people I knew. It was by far about the level of self-development both of us had worked at achieving over the years and for me, that year in particular. Amaka was also by far more sophisticated by how the kids in the states would expect a girl in Africa would be. However, after a few video calls with some of her friends that were schooling the United States and Canada, I could see that they had similar orientations. She was also coming to school in the states the following year and I hoped we could get into the same college and even if we didn't, we could remain close friends in the states, as it would definitely be easier to link up over there.

Somewhere in the mix, Hadiza reached out with a call. She was feeling great and after I mentioned our travel plans, she was willing to go with us. Thanks to the nature of her work, she was quite the adventurous type, so she was willing to travel as soon she could check her schedule and confirm that there was no work in her way. We were curious about the work with her new brand and I could feel her about to explode with joy over the phone as she talked about how amazing the deal was. She kept thanking us for the role we played when she was really down, and while we were happy, Amaka and I had been having fun all along such that everything we had done with her so far was not even much of a big deal left to us. She said she had bought a couple of things from her trips round France and we could come and check out clothes, jewelry and perfume we would like in the house the next day. She also said we could have a slumber party and just have fun altogether when we came.

Of course, you cannot have all three amazing women like us under the same roof with booze and a swimming pool with maximum fun. We had the most fun on that particular night and Hadiza had brought such amazing items that also made our nights. We talked all night especially about my experience in Lagos and people's various questions about if I was from Nigerian descent. There were also several stories about how men tried to warm their way up to me, but Amaka had warned me earlier about how Nigerian men would do anything to get US citizenship. Hence, all love stories were cancelled for me from the very beginning of the trip; for my own good of course. I did not want to become one of the several women around the world that had grudges against men for outsmarting them when they had fallen in love.

Luckily, I scaled through being blindsided by love, but of course, I had a lot of tea for my friends. It was a night if lots of laughter too. Hadiza also had tea for us about what happened during her various trips all over the world. The men of course, were the top of her stories. Men were men all over the world; doing anything and everything to warm their way up and get an experience of a beautiful woman's body. Well, my girl made sure to enjoy Paris in all the ways she could. She was in her early 20's anyway. All night, Amaka played the role of the aunty that judged what we did wrong, what we did right and how we would have made the best of certain situations. We listened of course, right until we realized that she hadn't spilled any tea. Then, my girl told me that Mr. Andrew was trying to find his way to get a piece of her. Well, she wasn't a minor. It was funny that I wasn't shocked. I never saw him as the lover boy type from the start. Now, he had done my bidding yet I also just got the ultimate ticket to blackmail him into getting absolutely nothing out of our deal. He was definitely a bad player; he shouldn't have tried that with my friend. She said it had been at the very start of our visit to Nigeria and he probably never imagined that we would get that close. Anyway, she didn't care about what happened to his love life, just as she wasn't interested in his advances from the start.

"I even totally forget that happened. I did not count him as a potential one, if you know what I mean."

"…but that's real tea." I said, as we clinked our glasses of champagne and said cheers.

At the end of the night, we got the best news ever as Hadiza offered to sponsor every other part of our trip apart from our tickets. It was the best news ever and I could not be more grateful about how my year was going. It was only getting better by the day. With my girls with me, our trip to Cape Verde was probably going to be the best trip of my life. No work, no obligations to anyone or anything; just three young women on a vacation to have fun. I had never had such. I had experienced holiday trips with my mum and some other trips with my siblings and their families (as they had sponsored it), but that was about it for us. That was really everything and now, I had gotten a chance to experience more.

Hadiza was such a freak when it came to shopping. She asked that we do yet another round courtesy of her. She talked about how she would have lost her life in this year and how things had gone so bad for her in every area of her life in this year, all for all every of her misfortunes to come together and give her the best news of her life.

"After all, if I am no more, then there would be no shopping. Pick some clothes ladies. Let's get to shopping." She had said.

I was glad that she was happy and more than ever, I realized how it was important to have the right kinds of friend in life. Life gets really messy. Life is not perfect at all, but having the right company gives you the right support system you need to have an amazing life. At random times, I remember giving them random hugs and kisses. I felt really safe doing all these; I felt really wanted by my friends. There was no deceit with them. We all truly loved each other. Hadiza had also realized that all the friendships she had in the media was a sham. She really treated us like gold; pure gold.

Cape Verde was everything we had read about and thought it would be, and then, some more. The beaches were as turquoise blue as we had seen in the pictures and videos online and maybe even more beautiful, It was a nice way to unwind considering the fact that all we had been hearing in the past few weeks were sad stories about cancer and the people we had been seeing were really sad too and we had to cheer them up with our own happy. Dear reader, I don't know about you, but personally, I really believe that energy is everything and as for Amaka and I, we had to use our happy energy to make those we came across happy to. The truth of what I am trying to tell you is that we were drained and we really needed to just relax non-stop that way and not feel guilty for it. Cape Verde was perfect for that. You may be of the opinion that we had been having fun all along in Nigeria, but trust me, nothing beats travelling all the way to such a beautiful place, knowing that you are going there just to have some fun. Your body, your soul and your future would thank you for such an experience. I have no doubts when I say this, especially if you choose a place as beautiful as Cape Verde.

We had booked an Airbnb from time, so once we got to the Island, we knew where we were headed to spend our two weeks. As for Hadiza, it was just an avenue for her to travel and not work, but just enjoy life and have reasons to be thankful of the gift that her life was. I was truly happy to have met her. You never know where you would meet amazing friends that would make your life better. However, I won't tie our becoming friends to only chance. All through my stay in Lagos, Nigeria, well, I never met anyone else from our volunteer group that groomed them as well as Amaka and me. We did not joke with things as seemingly simple as grooming and dressing. Our nails were always done, hair was always in good condition and when it came to dressing, our clothes were always crisp and clean. We looked nice and people loved to be associated to people that look nice. It is even a concept that s subconscious for most people. They don't even know why they are drawn to you. It is just always usually a matter of, "I want to be close to that girl right there. Who is she? I would like to know her." Even those richer than you would naturally feel comfortable around you because they would feel like you look like you are one of them, so you are definitely not looking to scam them. You know, the world in which we live forces the rich to be very protective of their company and they cannot be blamed for this.

It is the same concept that makes some people get better treatment than others. Think of it; of course, you are naturally wired to treat a person who is better dresses, better looking and better smelling with more respect because important people carry themselves in a manner that shows that they are important (well, at least about 90% of them). When a person looks shabby, you don't even necessarily want to have anything to do with them except it's a thing of compulsion. You don't even want to make friends with them. Hence, I believe this is a concept everyone can tap into. I am not talking about being a fraud and just being someone who you are not in public. I am talking about being dressed exactly how you want to be addressed and that is a very straightforward concept that anyone can grasp. If you want to be treated nicely, you really have to look the part, there are no shortcuts around it. If you go a club or a party looking shabbily, you won't be seated by the ushers or coordinators in a nice place. You are going to be seated away from the spotlight because you are not dressed properly, irrespective of how rich you may be. I have seen this over and over.

The exception to this would be if you are Mark Zuckerberg; in this case everyone knows you and the fact that you are not exactly the type that likes to dress up, and this would be fine by everyone, but if no one knows you or how much you may be worth, you really have to dress the part. Even if people know who you are or what you have, it really wouldn't hurt to look good. Even the queen of England still dresses the part. Royalty does not joke with what they wear and if you want to be treated like royalty, well, now you know exactly what to do. I am glad that Amaka and Hadiza shared the same beliefs, as they had also seen this work first hand. For this reason, my girls and I did not joke with our looks all day every day. We really made sure we looked good right from our time at the airport to coming down to Cape Verde and doing all the activities we did. We found that so many people wanted to relate to us or just do nice things for us because of how good we looked. Well, it was yet another time to see what we believe play out yet again. All the bikini, beach wear and perfume Hadiza had got played a huge role in all of this. We did not get to pay for a lot of things at Cape Verde because people really wanted to be associated with us. It was fun to watch and each time we got back to our make-shift home, we had reason to smile and laugh over and over. Humans were really very predictable.

They say Cape Verde which actually consists of up to 10 Island comes with lots of life, love and laughter. And it really did for us. We did not know that we would be split up that afternoon of ours at Boa Vista. It had many beaches and we just decided to wander off without each other. My friends and I had really been having fun together; swimming, jumping in the Boa Vista sand dunes, the traditional dancing and spotting the whales. However, more than ever, we realized that we were also at the perfect location to just wander off and think about life and all that it is. We all had our personal experiences with life and while being together was awesome, being alone at the beach with your thoughts is pure bliss. Gladly, we all believed this. However, it was all Hadiza's idea at first and more than anyone, we knew what she had to go through in this year in particular. She really deserved that space and quiet. As my friends wandered off and I strolled towards the other end of the beach, which I could not reach anyway, the thought of being alone with my thoughts in this beautiful location excited me. I could finally get to sit with my thoughts and just process the series of unexpected events that had happened to me this year; you know, just take in everything and see all the many reasons I have to be thankful for the gift of unpredictability that life usually came with. There was no better time to be thankful than that particular time. Who knew I would be having a time of my life like this, in this year.

I really thought about the fact that I was growing too, as I was usually the type that went on holidays and all I thought about was taking pictures for the gram. This time, I had taken pictures for the gram too, but I had not posted them because I was enjoying the moment too much to actually post in that particular moment. I guess that's what adults do. Well, the other reason I had not posted was that I did not want my mom or anyone at all to know I was at Cape Verde until I was back. If anyone else found out, it may circle back to my mom knowing and I did not want to give her any reason to worry about me or why I had gone on vacation to Islands in Africa all of a sudden. She would definitely be worried, especially because she had not seen me in almost two months. I could understand what her worries would be. At this point, I still sat at the bank of the beach, staring at the waves do their thing. It was fun to watch, how each wave trusted the other to carry it. I wished humans could be like that; perhaps, this way, we would be able to rest from our several struggles to do this or do that in life, because we can trust that the next person would make our lives easier and this way, we would be more rested and allow life to take its normal cause.

I don't know how it happened, but I found myself thinking about what I really wanted to do with my life, as I knew my major should be a determining factor for what course I took when I got into the university. As I thought, I said to myself, "I hate hospitals" and I instantly knew that I was lying because I now loved to relate with sick people and see what I could do to make them feel better and even if that had to happen within the four walls of a hospital, I did not mind at all. I just wanted to be of help and I thought it would be fun to help sick people for the rest of my life. Although, I did not know if that meant being a doctor, a nurse, a pharmacist, a physiotherapist, a radiographer or anything else in the medical field yet, at least I knew the path I now wanted to tow and I did not think that was such a bad place to get started. I now totally got what it is that people used to say about just living and following the path life keeps mapping out for you while being the best you can. In doing this, you would truly find what makes your heart beat, you would find what resonates with your soul and just makes you happy without having to try hard.

While caring for the sick or seeing how I could interact and help them, a sense of purpose always enveloped me so much that I did not care so much about what was happening outside where I was caring for the patients in that moment. That was all I could focus on in such moments and doing that made me very happy. I felt a sense of purpose flushing me as I thought of the entire journey of getting to this point in my life. I felt peace, I felt joyful. Then, in a blink of an eye, I could see my friends coming in a distance, they were waving at me. I waved right back before noticing that there was a young man behind me who had been trying to get my attention all the while. However, I had not heard him or noticed him. I was too lost in my own happy thoughts; it was almost unbelievable for me. Who ever thought that so early on, I would get to this point in my life where I did not really care much about attracting men or if I had a relationship? However, my guess is that this is what happens when you begin to walk in and you totally embrace your purpose.

This was not me doing the cliché of I want to focus on my life. For real, I had not been thinking much about the fact that I was not seeing anyone. I did not know that it was really possible to get to this stage where you do not truly get bothered about when your next relationship would be and maybe I was really too young to be thinking this way. I was supposed to be having fun and probably not remembering the name of the last person I kissed or the bar where I had met them. Honestly, I was having so much fun at all I was doing that I had entirely forgotten that there was another important part of life like that where you could really be in love with someone and enjoy their company while being very romantic with each other. I guess I had now found a new love in my purpose and you know how being new in a relationship feels; you could forget everyone else if you don't watch it. You could forget your friends and be entirely focused on your lover even if it is totally unintentional. This line of thinking made me realize that I had not called Diane and I also had not called Fiona to see how they were doing or fill them in on my activities. My phone had been on airplane mode all the while since I knew Mr. Andrews had me covered with my mom. I just wanted to have fun without caring about anything else for a bit. However, now, I also knew that I was so in love with the idea of my purpose that I had not called people that were so important to me. I promised myself to do that later that evening as he was now walking closer to me, seeing that I had actually turned to notice him. He was dark and tall. He was good looking too. I had always been a fan of black guys who looked like basketballers, so I decided that I was going to ask him if he was one or if he was ever going to be one once he approached me. What I did not notice while staring at him walk closer was that my friends were already with me too.

"Alright, we would just leave you two and catch up with you maybe back in the apartment." Hadiza said.

"Yes, that's right." Amaka said, turning awkwardly.

"No…" I said, trying to call out to them, but it was obviously too late as they were walking really fast. I knew that they were doing this on purpose, so I just shook my head. It was what I would typically do to a friend and it was quite a wonder to see that I now had friends that would do the same to me.

"Later girl." They shouted from a distance.

I was still looking at them walk away when his cool voice got my attention, "It looks like your friends approve to you getting to know me."

"Uhum."

His eyes were so innocent. You know how it is usually said that the eyes are the window of his soul? Yes, I believe in that and I could see that his soul was pure. So, when he said that they made amazing lobsters that were to die for somewhere close, I jumped at the idea of getting to know him over lobsters and cocktails without thinking much. Mind you, I did that because I could tell that he was a good person, not because I like food, as someone like Diane or even Fiona would probably think.

Okay, I love food, but of course, that is not the only reason I jumped at the offer of food from a total stranger.

"But you are a total stranger." I said as we walked towards the restaurant.

"I don't think you felt that way when you decided to come with me." He said smiling.

Oh, he was right. I could not deny it. I jumped at the offer like he was a friend. I could only smile.

"Trust me, you would like the food. And I also think it would be boring to get to know me if we are not eating or drinking. And I hate to bore a beautiful lady." He said.

Well, he was really smooth. We sat to eat and the lobster was really to die for. He told me that lobsters there were quite a classic and lobster restaurants were quite a big deal there. He was right. The lobster was amazing and as for the tall and handsome wonder, his name was Kofi and he was from Ghana. However, he lived in Senegal and ran a non-profit for cancer patients who did not have enough money to finance their treatment. This opened up a very long conversation between us two because it looked like the universe had done its thing to make us meet. We had so much to discuss thanks to our common ground and I was glad to share my many stories of my experiences with cancer patients. He also had stories to tell and four hours later, we were still at the lobster restaurant trying different things on their menu and chatting away without knowing that we had spent so much time together. Apparently, both of us were very in love with what we were doing and we were happy to meet another person that felt the same way about something so specific is such an unexpected location.

Senegal was very close to Cape Verde, so he came around from time to time to Cape Verde to enjoy the beaches, and unwind away from people. He also saw the serene environment as an opportunity to get ideas for the projects he was working on or ones he just planned to work on. I was really happy to meet him and I let him know that. So, there was Kofi, another solid friend added to my list.

On getting home, you could trust my friends to make me feel like I had met the love of my life.

"Gabriella, it's time to start spilling the tea on why you've been away from us for the past five hours and it had better be really interesting." Amaka said, as she had Hadiza came to sit with me on the table. I could only smile as I said, "Guys, what are you talking about?" Of course I knew what they were talking about.

"Such a handsome young man approaches a beautiful young woman and they spend hours together. Please, we are here for all that happened. After all, we gave you all that space." Hadiza said, and Amaka nodded in agreement.

"Guys…." I said, as I got on my feet and began to laugh. My friends looked at each other.

"Gabby, we are not joking. It had better be a good one, with all this laughter." Amaka said.

"Oops…you even seem more excited about this than me."

I was sorry to disappoint my friends. I knew I was going to disappoint them with this one as it was going to be boring to them, as our conversation had not progressed in the romantic direction. I was really sorry because I knew they expected better content from me.

"You won't believe me." I said.

"Did he propose or say he loves you already? I hate creepy guys." Said Hadiza.

"You are thinking too far. Nothing close to that. Our conversation did not even go that way." I said.

"Then, why did you guys spend so much time together?" Amaka seemed worried already.

"Because we were doing what people who just met do?"

"…and what is that?" Hadiza asked.

"We were talking." Both my friends stood up and began to walk away. They were apparently disappointed.

"That's boring." Said Hadiza.

"However, you won't believe that he runs an NGO in Senegal for cancer patients and he wants us to come to Senegal with him in two days."

"Now, that's what I'm talking about!" Hadiza exclaimed.

My girls liked the idea of a good travel and the fact that Kofi was even sponsoring the trip made it even better. I told them about our conversations and while they admitted that it was very coincidental that we were doing similar things, the thought of the trip in two days made them so happy. After all, our time in Cape Verde was supposed to be over in three days, so it was no travelling sacrificing only one extra day of the payment Hadiza had already made for another adventure.

Now, I knew had to put a call through to my girls at home. I had really been something really close to an asshole. I had not kept up with them since the time I left. As for Diane, she would have learnt one or two things from mom who was very much in contact with Mr. Andrews. So, my major concern and my first call was to Fiona. I needed to know how she was doing and also fill her in on all I had been doing. Perhaps, it would brighten up her mood.

It was a long call with Fiona. She sounded a bit down, but excitement kicked in when I started telling her about all my escapades; how Mr. Louis had dashed us some money and how we had decided to go Cape Verde, but Hadiza (which I just introduced as another rich friend for the sake of her privacy) was sponsoring every other expense asides that of our ticket. My friend was really happy to hear that all these had happened for me, but the excitement over the phone was short-lived per time. I knew she was just trying to be happy. I could hear it in her voice and wished there was something else I could do to help; so I kept dishing out one gist after the other, hoping that she would just feel better. She would only laugh for a while and then stop. The cycle continued over and over. It was only when I gave up on trying, as I did not want to ask direct questions about her dad (as she had instructed), that she told me that her dad had passed two days ago. She said her aunties came around and the burial would be really soon. I was sad that I would not be there with her to see her lay him to rest. It was because of all the plans to join Mr. Andrews back in Nigeria on his way back to the US. My friend was now an orphan and I couldn't be there for her. I cried my eyes out immediately I dropped the phone. I knew I had not said or done enough to console her, but there wasn't much I could do. It had happened and I could not take away the pain. I could just be there for her in my human way and you know we humans are very limited.

I was so sad all through the night while my friends tried to console me to no avail. My vibe was just off. I could not call Diane that night anymore. I called her the next morning and she had good news for me. She had passed her SAT and mom let her go to California for the weekend, to spend time with her boyfriend. It was a video call so she let me see him as a surprise and it was an amazing conversation with them both. I made sure to fill them in with all my adventures and we laughed and laughed. However, I had to break the sad news to her. She and Fiona had gotten very fond of each other since the latter came to the house often to see me. She was truly sorry and promised to reach out. It was the best we could all do at the time, but she promised to be home in time to attend the burial.

Me and my girls were literally living the life. This was the idea of friendship I had dreamt of all my life; one in which every member of the group is actually an addition. I liked the fact that thanks to one of us, all of us could benefit even more at every point. Staying over at Amaka's place, Hadiza paying for our Airbnb and now, I had a friend who was going to take us to Senegal, all expense were to be paid at that. He was especially excited about the fact that we knew about cancers. His NGO was supposed to have a workshop to enlighten her members on cancers once again, as he complained that they were all burning out. So, he saw us and our coming to Senegal as an added advantage.

Kofi had said, "Look, if they hear all these stories you are telling me, they would be fired up to do more." He also noticed that I had so much passion for the work and kept saying his volunteers took the planning of their outreaches and sourcing for fund for granted too often.

It was as though he was the only one with fire among them, so each time he spoke, they literally made him feel like he was doing too much or saying too much. It made him feel crazy and he just thought that if they listened to me, they would know that there were people out there that really needed help and they would be fired up to work again. Honestly, I understood what he meant, I had never just understood it personally as it had never happened to me as a volunteer, but I had seen it happen to others. I could see the other volunteers that were all fired up during our six weeks training, but just burnt out all of a sudden. They were happy to work and help others and were all gingered up to work for the first few weeks too, but started slacking along the way. This never just happened for me personally. The more I worked and met new patients, the more I wanted to meet more and just encourage them to keep going in spite of their condition.

I was surprised that Kofi thought I was a serious one. I never saw myself that way. Honestly, I still saw myself as that same last child that just wanted to enjoy life, so it was strange for somehow to see me that way; as a serious person. However, while we were still hanging out within those four hours and I brought up how my friend, Amaka, and I were always so concerned about each new patient, he put it to me that we were serious chaps. I kept disagreeing saying that we were fun-loving young girls and we only loved to help people and put smiles on faces. He still disagreed. This was what made me think over everything as I lay down to sleep that night, and as I thought, I realized that we were actually serious at our volunteer work. We were always determined to effectively help every patient we came in contact with. However, we were still those fun-loving girls that dressed so well and looked pretty always. I guess we were really living proofs that as a young girl, you could really be anything. People usually put young ladies in boxes; they give us stereotypes. You have to be beautiful or smart; you can't be both. They make it seem like a miracle when you are both or they simply turn their eyes away when they see the other parts of you, all because they don't want their theories to be proved as wrong. They were bent on being right, of course.

"Then, who is the third lady?" he asked. Her face looked quite familiar, but I could not exactly place from where. Then, I pulled out my phone and showed him her picture again.

"Wow! I know her face from a billboard and even though I cannot remember the name, she is that model who had lots of social media trouble this year." He said.

"Social media trouble?"

"Of course I don't want to bring up the details."

"Oh, yes. I get it."

"…and boy, did she have cancer."

"…and it made her life better."

"She should definitely speak to my volunteers." He said, and I nodded in agreement.

My friends were excited about the free trip to the popular Dakar, Senegal. They did not know the details and I decided to keep that as a surprise. It was probably wrong of me to do so to Hadiza in particular, but I did not want her to chicken out on something she could actually do. It was something that would help other people become better at what they did. I really wanted them to inspire those volunteers and I was sure that it was an experience she would eventually be grateful for. Let's just say I acted in the stead of her management for the time being. Kofi was going to be busy with the details of the workshop throughout the next day and I was going to spend the day with the girls alone, so there was no how they were going to know the details of the trip through a discussion with him. It was going to be a real adventure for the girls because the first time they would hear of their roles in this workshop with about 70 people in attendance was going to be on the flight to Dakar, Senegal. They would probably scream, get mad at me briefly and eventually do it. We only had to talk about our experiences and encourage the volunteers that the work they were really doing mattered and could actually save a life.

The day to leave came and we were on our way to the airport. Kofi had made the process seamless for us and as we got on the plane, he began to talk to Amaka and Hadiza, asking for what their plans were with speaking the volunteers in Dakar the next day and the day after that.

"Speaking to the volunteers?" Hadiza asked confused.

"You didn't tell them?" Kofi asked rhetorically.

This was the part where I got to play dumb, but Amaka was sure to call my attention to issue properly.

"Begin to explain." She said, tapping me lightly.

"Kofi, sorry for the whole mix up. It is our friend here that has to do the explaining." Amaka apologized before turning back to me.

"I thought we were going to Dakar to have fun."

"Of course, there are plans in place for that." Kofi reassured us. He had noticed what had happened and he just did well to give the side eye for not telling my friends.

"Well…we would just be talking to the volunteers about our experiences with cancer and seeing cancer patients generally." I said.

"Oh…amazing." Hadiza said, giving me the side eye. "We would talk about this privately once we get off the plane." I assumed that the remaining 1 hour of our 1 hour 20mins flight would be very quiet between all of us and I just hoped that was enough time for my friends, especially Hadiza to cool off. She was obviously not very pleased by what I had done.

When we got to our hotel and we came down to the lobby for drinks as agreed, was when Hadiza finally talked to me. "I don't have an issue talking to the volunteers. You should have just told me ahead of time. I hate to be caught unawares like that." she said. As for Amaka, she kept giving me the side eye and I knew that she would keep doing that for quite a while. She would cool off when she was ready. However, I still had to apologize to the both of them for what I had done. It was the noble thing to do, considering the fact that I really did not seek their consent.

"I am sorry girls. I just really did not want you guys to bail on this trip. You are in Africa, you can always come here later. As for me, I cannot come here later like you guys. And I did not want to come here alone. So, his idea to bring you here to just talk about your experiences while being on a fully-funded trip sounded good to me."

"Did you say you did not want to come here without us?" asked Amaka.

"I think I heard that too." Said Hadiza.

At this, they came to give me a mushy hug, calling me their baby. I could wrap my head around Hadiza saying that, but Amaka was only two months older than me, so that was definitely not working for me from her end.

I liked how we could get over a disagreement after a level of basic understanding. After our discussion, at least we could go on with the day as it was just noon and we had only come for a smoothie. Kofi came to pick us up and off we went to the largest monument in Africa and the second largest in the world. It is called the African Renaissance Monument and it is a symbol of defiance and future prosperity. The statue on it which is of a man, woman and a child is also the tallest statue in Africa. It was indeed a wonder and it is located right outside Dakar, Senegal. It was finished up in the year 2010 and was definitely a wonder to see. Right inside it was a museum which had a lot that talked about the history of Africa. It really felt great to come to such a historic sight and I took a lot of pictures for Diane and Fiona. Perhaps, when things die down, I would also be able to tell my mom the story of all my escapades and eventually show her the pictures of all the beautiful places her baby girl had been to. They say Senegal is the gateway to Africa and I loved it there. The people seemed very peaceful. They loved fun too, but not in the loud way the people of Lagos, Nigeria liked to have fun. I could honestly say that both places were fun places, just in different ways and in ways that would suit different personality types.

We ate the traditional foods and also drank a traditional white drink that looked like a smoothie. It actually tasted really good, but had such a weird name. It was called the monkey bread drink, as they say it is made from monkey bread. Very weird, I would say. I asked for another cup anyway, whatever a monkey bread meant.

The next day was the day of the workshop and the young volunteers who were about my age and a few probably a little older listened with rapt attention as I spoke about my own experience. They seemed inspired and it was surreal to me that I could be the one to inspire some people across the world to do great things. I was trying hard to do the whole African accent thing and speak my English as they did, but they chorused back saying they liked my American accent. That was such a funny moment. Amaka came up and I saw them listen and take notes too. Wow! My friends and I were really making impact. We were really just girls that set out to have fun, so it was all still surreal.

Hadiza was the last to speak and when she came up, they roared. They had not really seen her before. She had experienced cancer on a very important organ of her body—her skin. Her own story was different; peculiar to herself. I could see a couple of them wipe their eyes as she spoke. This was a story they had seen on social media; her life had been out there in the public, so hearing her talk about it meant a lot. I shed a tear and it was a tear of joy about the amount of strength my friend was exuding. Additionally, I was happy that I was part of the process. She made sure to mention how we were the volunteers that helped her and were now her friends. Our friendship and individual testimonies now stood as a proof to them that the volunteering actually made a difference. I could only hope the words we spoke would stay with them. As expected, they came up to us after the workshop, asking how to handle different dilemmas and more on our experiences. We were happy to share. We were not the only speakers; there were other amazing speakers and different activities in between. In fact, we also benefitted from the entire concept. It was a honor to be part of the whole thing.

CHAPTER FOURTEEN

I woke up literally satisfied on my third day in Dakar. We were to leave Dakar on that day in particular. I woke up earlier than my friends on that morning and I stared at my blessings. Yes, my friends were blessings and I could not be grateful enough for the amazing things we had done together. For what we had achieved in Dakar all while having fun, I was thankful too. They were the sweetest ever, they were the kindest and by far the most understanding. They were also mature and I thought about the fact that if I did not come to Africa, I would never have met them. It would have been a real shame, to have not met such amazing souls. They woke up and we decided to go have some fun in the pool before our flight which was for later in the day. Hadiza had been a rebel all along. Her management had been calling her for media rounds, but she had decided that she just needed to have her fun and her space for the time being. She did not want the noise or the fakeness that came with the whole media thing. She did not want to have to put up an act for at least a while. She did not want to smile if she was not really in the mood, like a job required her to do. So, she totally turned off her phone to avoid feeling guilty and then, she got another phone with which she could talk to family. She had settled her family in all the ways she was supposed to and she had now setup her mom even in a bigger way than she had thought she would, thanks to the massive deal her misfortune had helped her to close. She was at peace with herself and I could see that. It even made her glow better.

Sometimes, you really just meet people that are in your life to help you on your journey to purpose. Kofi and I knew that this was what our relationship was for. We went for a couple of dates and it was all about purpose. Love is really beautiful and a happy relationship is indeed everyone should desire. However, there is more to life. Dear reader, this is probably not what you are expecting to hear as at least every story like this one should have a bit of love in it. Yes, I might have experienced a bit of that here and there, but there is always a conviction about the season of your life in which you are at every point. For me, I knew for sure that I would find love, but this was not the time. This was just the time I lived and enjoyed everything that life was. Not every amazing meeting at romantic location turns into a love story and that is fine. He was such an inspiring young man and I was glad to be able to be of help in terms of giving inputs on the development of his non-profit organization.

As for love and an amazing relationship, I knew it would come at the right time. I was really that black girl that turned heads. I am 5 feet 9 inches tall and I have my mama's hour glass figure and a full afro. Maybe my curves were not as amazing as my mum's, but I knew that I would get there as I grew. However, I got a lot of attention in high school, so that was not even the problem. Life was really just in stages and this was something I understood deeply for myself and a principle I never joked with, not even for a day. I think we would save ourselves lots and lots of heartaches as young people if we understood the seasons of our lives.

I spent the entire 3 hours and about 35 minutes of my flight from Dakar to Lagos reflecting on the year and everything that had happened in my life. I never imagined for once that I would be on a flight with people that I had known in less than two months, but felt like I had known on my life. I envisaged a year of fun and indeed I was having fun, but in an entirely different way than what I had thought to be my own idea of fun and ideal way of having fun. I was grateful for what I was experiencing in my own personal life. I used to be so superficial some months back, but a lot had indeed changed about me, I needed to admit. The things I cared about had changed and that included whatever people thought I was doing or if they thought I was wasting my time with whatever I was doing. I absolutely did not care.

We had done a lot in Africa. It was so surreal and I was really proud of what I had been doing.

"We have done a lot in Africa! I did it!" I screamed to Diane on my last video call to her before my flight. "I am coming home! I made you proud." Of course, Diane had been back at home for a bit and she was there when Fiona had laid her dad to rest. She had obviously missed me a lot and I kept thinking that this would have been her experience and not mine. However, I was really thankful that it was my experience. The little, inexperienced me had actually done something really good with the past few months. I had every reason to be proud. It was the super excellent kids in school who were also super serious that usually thought of being volunteers to Africa, but here I was, I had all that and I even enjoyed it and made amazing friends along the way.

Yes, I made amazing friends and this was why when it was time to leave, I could not hold back my tears. I could not wrap my heads around the fact that I would not be working with Amaka again. I liked Africa because of the amazing people I had met. Amaka was going to come to school in the states the following year and I also planned to go into college then too. I could only hope that we would not be so far away from each other. She was certainly the kind of friend I wanted to keep in my life for a long time. As for Hadiza, her movement was unpredictable, but she came to the US every now and then, so we could only hope that work could spare her some time to be with me whenever she was in my state or city. We promised each other to keep being in touch and we sadly said our goodbyes as we had to.

"We did that! We helped people and we had fun. We did that girls!" Amaka said, apparently having a lot of feelings running with the blood in her veins, as she kept pecking Hadiza and I back and forth. We laughed at this and we could see a couple of people in the airport staring at us and probably wondering what was making us super happy. However, we did not still care. They could think all they want; we had found something rare with each other. We had found true friendship and for me, while at it, if not all, I knew I had found a very important portion of my purpose and I was grateful for that.

Do I love hospitals now? Well, who cares? I hardly cared about the location any longer. As long as it was an avenue to help people, especially what had become my specialty, cancer patients, you could count me in. I would be more than happy to help irrespective if it was in or outside a hospital. Here's what I found about places: different places meant different things to different people. As a child, hospitals made me think of injections and pain. Hospitals reminded me of drugs, their bitter taste and their horrible smell. So, I hated hospitals. To the child of any healthcare professional, their dad or mum's office in the hospital was probably a place of comfort for them. What I am saying is that we interpret what places mean to us as we decide what those places actually mean to us. At the moment, I knew better. I knew that I had to make an appointment with the doctor if I feel unwell and I need to feel better. I know that I have to go to the hospital to also do my work as a volunteer and in that case, I had no reason to hate hospitals.

"Look at me. Who ever thought that my way of looking at these things will change?" I whispered to myself as the flight took off.

"What's that?" Mr. Andrews, who sat beside me, asked. I only smiled and turned away from him. If he had looked properly, he would have seen that it was a fake smile. I wondered why he was sitting beside me. To save me in the case of a plane crash in a bid to win my mother's heart? Now, he had no way around it since he had been trying to be with Amaka too. What a shame!

I was imagining how shocked he would be when I told him all I knew. I had told Diane about the Amaka situation and she told me how she had seen Fiona differently and they had been trying to distract her by talking about other issues. It turns out he had made moves on Fiona too and had promised to come see her when he was back. Fiona was not interested in the old man from the start, but he won't keep pushing. Now that I had more evidence, I decided that I would just talk to him myself so he would totally pull away from my mother by not making any further moves on her when he was back. He had been useful all those times I had put my phone on "Do not disturb" at parties, but now, show time was really over and I felt sorry for him. Or maybe I didn't. It was quite obvious that he did not know what he had skills to go round for all the ladies. My dear Mr. Andrews was about to lose what he had been working for with my mother, as I was coming for him strongly and I hoped he would be strong enough too.

My time on the plane back home was a time of reflection and a time to draw conclusions. What if Diane had not wanted to take the SATs? What if she had spoken to someone else and not? What if I had continued to be adamant with my various excuses about not working in a hospital? Perhaps, I would just party all year long, but when all that was over, would I be able to say I had truly experienced any satisfaction? Will my fears really have held back all these opportunities, of which the chief of them was all that I had learnt and then become? It was as if all those my initial fears did not exist any longer. They had not told us that we would most likely not need all those transfer skills, CPR and other skills taught to us. No, we would not need them, except in very extreme situations. They did not tell us our work was going to be pretty much fun, but probably not for everyone, because some people ended up pulling out, but not me. I could not imagine leaving it all and just going back to my chilled life like it was all a dream. I couldn't just imagine it. Who knew I would stay up to this moment—the sixth month. I had really thought I would get tired and not fit in. I thought I would pull out real soon, but here I was, wanting to continue to volunteer and truly being one of the bests at it. Life was so unpredictable and even we humans are unpredictable. We cannot say what we would like or fall in love with sooner or later. We could say the little we know, but our knowledge is of course very limited to what we know in the moment. Especially when we are young, there is perhaps so much we are yet to discover about ourselves. The whole experience really taught me never to really close the door on anything in my life. I could imagine any other life that did not include all my adventures in the last six months, and especially, the last two months. Imagine not being able to meet amazing people like Amaka, Hadiza or Kofi. Also, imagine that they did not get a chance to meet me because I decided to just stay somewhere in the United States and generally not care about doing anything new. Just imagine. I would have denied myself the opportunity to really live my life to be fullest and my view of life would not be as broad as it currently was.

I knew when I was back, Diane would want to step up to her work and that was fine. I felt like my time doing the work was now over and it was time for me to step back and do all the resting and thinking I needed to do. I could have all the fun I needed to have while now figuring out what I wanted to do with my life. I knew all the figuring out would even be easier now since I had gotten the opportunity to just see life better.

Mom let Diane come get me from the airport. On sighting her, I literally leaped for joy and wrapped her in my embraced. Everything that I had experienced would not have happened if not for her.

"Thank you!" I exclaimed.

Then she had her proud moment for a bit. She shrugged. "You know, I go around doing nice things for people. This is nothing, okay?"

I gave her the side eye and then, we burst into laughter.

"Look at you, in love with my kind of thing!"

"No, this is just being human. This is the kind of work any human being should be able to fall in love with. It's been such an amazing experience."

"Omg! Who is this?" she said in a loud voice. "...because this is not my cousin from six months ago? What have you done to her? Please, return her to us, we love her so much."

"So, you don't like this 'grown' woman version of Gabby."

"Please, miss me on that grown woman stuff." She laughed.

Mr. Andrews was looking at me from a distance. My assumption was that he was waiting for his cab. However, his stare was one that connoted the fact that we had unfinished business with each other.

"One moment." I said to Diane as I excused myself and walked towards him.

"Won't you thank me for all my help while you travelled?"

"Exactly what I came to do sir. Thank you so much Mr. Andrews, the world feels better because there are people like you in it. My experience wouldn't be complete without the stories of how you covered up for me with my mom while I switched off my phone and just travelled out of Nigeria. I am very grateful for your help and I do not take it for granted." That was a whole ass speech I constructed right there and I was not even expecting it. Sometimes, talking non-stop was my way of pouring out my anger to an elder I did not want to be direct with. I hoped he would catch my drift, but I don't think he did. This made me wonder if he was just trying to ignore my body language.

"Of course, you know how to really thank me. You can simply say nice things about me to your mom, or what do you think? I would really appreciate you saying thank you that way."

"Oh…do you want me talking to her about how you are also interested in my friend, Amaka or my other friend, Fiona? If that is what you want, I have no problem doing that…sir."

He looked at me, shocked. He just kept staring and he was lucky enough to have his cab come just about that.

"I would take my leave now." He said, walking towards the cab while still looking at me shocked.

I just hoped he got the friendly memo and would forget my mom altogether.

It was at this point Diane started walking up to me, but this time she wasn't alone. I knew the other face was familiar, but it was until she was closer that I knew that it was Fiona. I hugged her hard. I was glad to see my friend. We had a lot of catching up to do and I could not wait for all three of us to be behind closed doors and alone already. After a bit of rest, it was indeed an amazing evening with my friends. I did video calls with Amaka and Hadiza respectively, telling them that I was home and introducing them to Diane and Fiona. I felt blessed indeed.

One thing I took away from the entire experience was that in helping others, you can help yourself too. I had so much clarity than I had six months back. I knew that whatever I did with my life had to be a career path that enabled me to work in the hospital, the same hospital I once hated. I had found myself while offering to be of help to other people; I had found all the help I needed too—the irony of life. The time Diane took over from me was just perfect. I was glad that I had that short time of learning and it was quite impactful. In purpose, it is not about the length of time, it is the impact you can draw no matter how short the timing is. I could have chosen to continue the work, but I knew that all I had to learn there was over. There is how you just know these things for sure and for me, I really knew.

As I bring this book to a close, I cannot help but think of my grandmother. She was such a strong woman, but who says she did not need any help. I cannot help but wonder if she actually got the support she needed. I wonder if things would have been any different if she had someone outside our amazing family that she could open up to. There was something about being the source of strength and beacon of hope for your family, even when you are down, you just want to keep doing your best, even at your own expense. This is not a good way to handle sickness especially. A sick person needs all the help and support they can get. Awareness was still an important issue, especially among males. As for my grandmother, she was a female like a male, always acting tough just to ensure that everyone in our extended family had that strong shoulder they could lean on since grandpa was no more. I just wondered if things would have been different if there was a volunteer like me talking to her. Perhaps, even if she still died (which she was probably bound to as her cancer was in its final stage when we discovered it), she would have died happier.